GRETA'S GOAT

A MORGAN'S FIRE ROMANCE

M. LEE PRESCOTT

Greta's Goat

By

M. Lee Prescott

Published by Mt. Hope Press
Copyright 2021, M. Lee Prescott
ISBN: 978-1-7352948-6-5
Istock.com/AjaKoska
encrier/Bigstock.com
Cover design: Ashley Lopez

http://www.mleeprescott.com/

This book is a work of fiction. Names, characters, places, and events are products of the author's imagination or are used fictitiously. Any resemblance to actual people (alive or deceased), locales, or events is entirely coincidental.

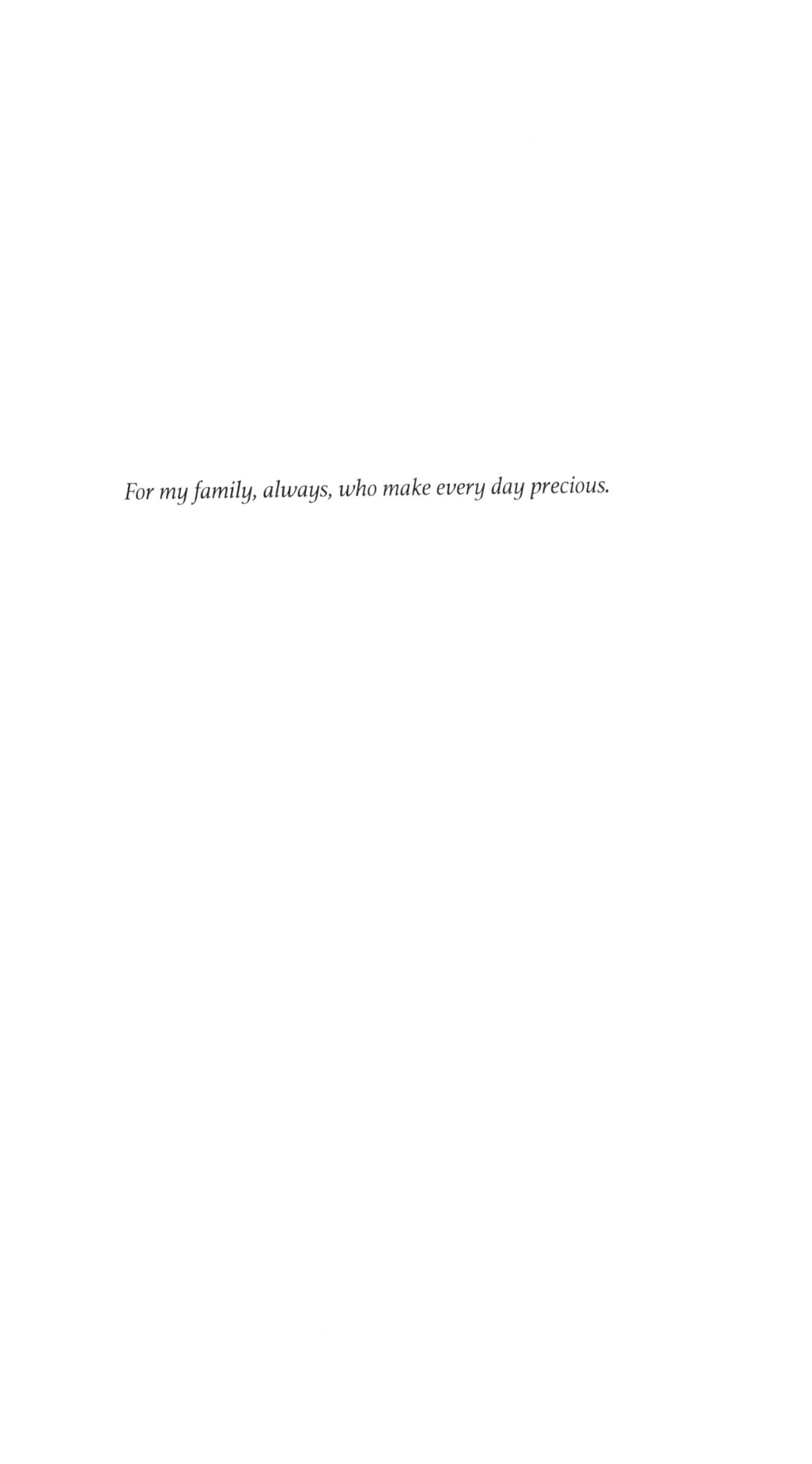

For my family, always, who make every day precious.

CHAPTER 1

"This is ridiculous," Greta Jeffers said aloud, pulling the leash attached to a Tennessee fainting goat.

"Nice, docile breed. Make good pets, and their meat is great," Tom Crocker said when he dropped the kid off. "Haven't named her yet. Thought you'd like to do the honors, Ms. Jeffers. Wouldn't recommend a name if you're considering the meat route."

Local farmer Tom Crocker was the parent of one of her students. Billy Crocker had had a difficult sophomore year and had spent a great deal of time in Greta's office. A social worker at Cove High School, Greta had received a number of end-of-the-year gifts from appreciative parents, but a *goat*? *Really?*

As her gift dug in her heels, Greta became more and more exasperated. Tom Crocker had just driven away, and she was attempting to lead the recalcitrant creature to her fenced-in backyard. Greta lived on the ocean in a small cottage left to her by her parents, both of whom had died in the past year. To say it had been a tough year was an understatement.

Lost in thought, she relaxed her grip on the leash for an instant, and that was all it took. The black-and-white creature reared back, pulled out of the leash and was off at a run, headed down the Coast

Road. "Dammit!" Greta cried, realizing she'd never be able to catch the thing. *Even with short stubby legs, it can move!*

She ran into the house, grabbed her keys and raced to her truck. The dark green Tacoma had been her dad's, and she said a silent prayer of thanks that she'd kept it and traded in her Honda. The goat was out of sight by the time she backed out into the road. There was a long track of open land in this section of the Coast Road, property of Cady Enterprises, owners of a very successful music venue, Sandy's, a mile south of Greta's home.

By the time she pulled up beside the goat, they were a quarter mile from Sandy's. "The little bugger," she muttered, driving past and parking in the club's large lot. She planned to head her off at the pass, so she jumped from the truck and hid at the corner of the sprawling complex. As the goat ran by, she leapt. "Gotcha!" she cried as the goat slipped from her grasp again and rounded the building.

"Whoa, little fella," a voice called.

Greta ran around the side of the club, coming face-to-face with Murph O'Neill, Sandy's manager. He had stepped on the leash and was bending to grab hold of it as she approached.

"Thank goodness!" Greta said as she reached them.

Murph smiled. "Yours?"

"Yes, I'm afraid so."

"Didn't figure you for a goat person."

"I'm not. She's a present from an appreciative parent." Greta knew Murph from town, but she'd had a memorable dinner with him when her friend and colleague Pam Morgan had been dating Murph's boss, Sandy Rodriguez, founder and former owner of the club. There had been an attraction there, but Murph had been dating Sadie Riley, a local yoga instructor. Horseshoe Crab Cove was a very small town,, so the attraction had gone no further. *Too bad he's as gorgeous as ever*, she mused.

The tall redhead was built like a brick shithouse. His brown eyes sparkled with mischief as he proffered the leash to her. "Sure you can handle her?"

"No, decidedly not. Don't suppose you'd like to help me get her into my truck?"

"Happy to," he said, leaning down and scooping up the tiny creature. "She's a cute little thing, isn't she?"

"Hmm, cute and naughty."

"What's her name?"

"Doesn't have one yet. I was advised not to name her if I eventually want to eat her."

He shot her a look. "What? You wouldn't!"

"No, I wouldn't. I'm not even sure I can keep her. What do I know about goats?"

Murph hoisted the animal into the back of her truck and looped the leash through a side bar to secure her. "How far do you have to go?"

"Just a mile or so." She pointed northward. "I live up the coast a bit."

"Lucky you. Listen, hang on. I'll follow you and help you get her wherever she's going. Whaddya say?"

He has the most beautiful caramel flecks in his eyes, she thought. Thirty seconds later, she realized she'd been staring and quickly found her voice. "I say yes, sure, that'd be great."

MURPH JUMPED INTO HIS JEEP AND SWUNG OUT OF THE LOT ONTO THE Coast Road. Greta had already pulled out and was waiting for him. He remembered Pam Morgan Rodriguez's friend and was surprised he hadn't seen her around the village lately. *Man, is she ever pretty!* Short and slender, she had a sharp, delicate beauty, with an oval face framing lovely blue-violet eyes and stylish short brown hair.

They pulled into her driveway side by side, and Murph hopped out, untying the goat and picking her up. "Nice place," he said, turning to admire the cottage and surrounding property. The tiny, shingled cottage, a barn/garage beside it, sat fifty yards from the cliffs overlooking the ocean beyond. Behind the house was a large fenced-in yard with verdant green grass, a garden shed, and beautiful gardens. Someone had taken loving care of this property. Murph wondered how the gardens would fare with a goat running free.

"It was my parents' home."

"What, did they move to Florida?"

"No, they both passed away this year."

"Gee, I'm sorry. Double whammy. That's gotta be rough."

"It was."

He glimpsed sadness reflected in her beautiful eyes and had the urge to set the goat down and hug her. *Poor kid.* "Where do you want this beast?"

"Backyard."

The four-foot split-rail fence was lined with almost invisible mesh wire. He wondered how big the kid would grow and whether an extension would need to be added to the top of the fence.

Greta closed the gate behind them and he set the goat free. It scampered around exploring, digging with her little hooves, sniffing flowers and eating the new buds and grass. "Oh, boy, so much for Mom's flower beds," she said, shaking her head.

"There might be something you can spray on them to discourage her."

"We'll see. Would you like something to drink?"

"I was going to ask if you'd had lunch," he said. "Figured you deserved a break after this ordeal."

Greta laughed, a throaty, genuine laugh. "Love to, but I probably shouldn't leave little Daisy Belle on her own till I figure out what I'm going to do with her."

"Probably smart," he said, figuring this was his exit cue.

As he turned, she said, "But I'd be happy to have you join me for lunch. We can eat out here on the terrace. On a whim, I cooked up a bunch of bacon this morning. I could make BLTs?"

He grinned. "Be my pleasure. Can I help?"

"What would be most helpful would be for you to stay out here and keep an eye on you-know-who."

"No problem."

"Iced tea or water?"

"Love the tea," he said, walking beside her to the terrace, where he sat on one of wrought iron chairs topped with comfortable canvas cushions.

Greta smiled. "Be right back. Don't let her eat every flower before I return."

OH BOY, GRETA THOUGHT AS SHE CARRIED THE TRAY WITH SANDWICHES, iced teas, and a bowl of handmade potato chips from the local bakery. *He's as cute as ever. Too bad he's got a girlfriend.* She'd been alone too long. Her last boyfriend, Hugh Koffman, a colleague at the high school, had flown the coop a year ago around the time of her mom's death. Then all hell had broken loose with her dad's illness, and thoughts of dating flew away along with Hugh. *What a jerk!*

"Here we go!" she said, setting down the tray. Murph was at the back of the yard trying to lure the kid away from the gardens with fistfuls of grass. "It's okay. Let her do what she wants while we eat. This afternoon, I'll google goat repellants or goat rescue."

He joined her at the table. "Thanks for this. It looks great and sure beats what's in Sandy's fridge until our cook gets in."

"The least I can do after all your help," Greta said, thinking what a wonderful smile he had. *Remember, he has a girlfriend!*

"You know, she might be okay and leave the plantings alone once she gets her own food. So are you gonna call her Daisy Belle?"

"Maybe just Daisy. Temporarily, till I figure out where she's going."

"You could check around. Maybe they'd take her to Land's End or Morgan's Fire," he said, referring to two local farms.

"I'll ask Pam if she thinks they'd want her. Weezie Morgan runs pony camps, and I heard she was thinking about starting some 4-H programs."

Murph chuckled. "Goats and bunnies. I loved 4-H."

"I'm afraid I never did 4-H or any other animal husbandry training."

"You'll be fine. Where're you gonna keep her at night? Temporarily, I mean, until you find a home."

"Oh, gee, I hadn't thought. I guess it'll have to be the shed. I'll clean things out this afternoon."

They enjoyed their sandwiches, chatting about her work and the club and who was performing that night.

"Oh, I love them," she said when he mentioned that the Mitch Corcoran group was playing. "We saw them in Newport last year."

"Yup, they draw a huge crowd. You should come, if you can leave little Daisy. I'll tell them to comp you at the door."

"Thanks, but I'm not much for going to clubs alone. If I can wrangle someone into coming, I'll see."

"Hope you do," he said, taking the last bite of his sandwich. "That was the best BLT I've ever had."

"Thanks. So how is it working at Sandy's without Sandy? Do you miss him?"

"Yup, but this is probably temporary, working for Cady. Elizabeth, the owner, is supposed to be headhunting for my replacement. She offered me the job and a ridiculous salary to go with it, but it's not the same without the boss. A couple of us feel that way, and when the restaurant is ready to open, we all have jobs." He referred to his former boss's newest venture, a farm-to-table called Field and Fire, located near the Morgan's Fire winery on the vast property owned by Richard Morgan.

They sat sipping their teas, watching Daisy roam the yard. "She is pretty cute, isn't she?" Greta said.

Murph laughed. "Sure is. So you're looking at free labor? That shed's not gonna clear itself out."

Surprised, she gazed over at him. "Didn't you have anything to do today?"

He grinned. "Can't turn my back on a damsel in distress. Two damsels in distress." He pointed to Daisy.

"Well, okay, then. It's kind of a disaster in there. Let's me put the lunch stuff in the kitchen and grab a broom and some trash bags."

He grinned. "Daisy and I'll be waiting."

CHAPTER 2

Greta and Murph worked steadily on the shed for several hours, Daisy occasionally peeking in. Most of the equipment housed in the shed was moved to the second bay of the barn that served as a garage. They hung some of the garden tools on hooks out of Daisy's reach.

Once the shed floor was swept, they stood back to admire their work. "You're gonna need some food and bedding," he said. "I'll drive in to Cove Feed and Grain. They'll have hay and also pine shavings for her bedding."

Greta was about to protest that he'd done enough, then decided she shouldn't leave Daisy to her own devices yet. "Are you sure you have time?"

"Yup."

"Have Mike bill me. I have a charge account there left over from my parents."

"Will do. In the meantime, you might want to google what plants are poisonous for goats and look around the yard. You've got a lot of ornamental bushes."

This is absurd, she thought as Murph drove off. *I don't have time to take care of a goat!*

Nevertheless, she hurried inside to grab her laptop and searched for harmful plants and food, then took an inventory of the yard. Thankfully, the holly trees and honeysuckle were outside the fence down in her parents' small orchard, and the azaleas were in the front facing the ocean.

When Murph returned, he quickly unloaded the bales of hay and shavings, as well as a twenty-five pound bag of grain. "Sorry, I gotta run and get set up for tonight," he said after depositing the last load in the barn. "You gonna be okay getting these out to the shed?"

"Absolutely. I can't thank you enough for giving up your day to help with my crazy, unexpected house guest."

He grinned. "My pleasure. It was fun. I grew up around lots of animals, and I miss it. Stop by tonight if you want."

"Thanks, but I think I'll make some phone calls and get Daisy settled in."

"Here's the slip from the supplies." Their hands brushed against each other as he handed her the receipt, and Greta was surprised at the electric feeling that coursed through her.

He met her gaze, a warm smile playing around his eyes. "Hey, we should grab dinner sometime."

"I'd like that," she heard herself say, even as warning bells sounded.

Murph hopped into his jeep, cranking down the window. "See you around, then. Good luck with Daisy. Goats are pretty easy, though they're jumpers, so watch that she doesn't jump the fence. They like companionship too, so you may want to think about getting her a buddy."

"I'm not listening," she said, as she waved goodbye.

AFTER WAVING TO MURPH, GRETA CIRCLED THE HOUSE TO THE backyard, where she found Daisy asleep in the shade at the edge of the back flower beds. Her tiny head rested between her hooves. *Adorable.* Four wheelbarrow loads later, she had hay and pine bedding spread in the shed. As she worked, Daisy woke and followed her, peering with curiosity into the shed, finally venturing in to nibble hay. Greta filled the water trough Murph had bought and set it just inside the shed door. She then sat on the floor and watched Daisy eat and drink, wondering how the baby goat would do all alone all night.

Finally, she headed inside to call Tom Crocker. His wife, Stephanie, answered. "Hey, Ms. Jeffers, how's the baby doing?"

"I was hoping to ask you about nighttime and what I can expect. I've cleaned out my shed and she has plenty of food and water, but I guess I'm wondering if she'll be lonely out there."

"Might be, but she'll get used to it. You might hear a bit of bleating tonight. First time she's been away from her tribe. She'll miss her mom and her brothers and sisters. Goats are social animals."

"I was afraid of that."

"Did Tom tell you she's house trained?"

"Really?"

"She was supposed to be for my youngest as a 4-H goat, so we let Ruby keep her in the house, but then Ruby took a shine to her kid brother, and Tom thought you might like our precious baby."

"Is she used to sleeping in the house, then?"

Stephanie chuckled. "On and off. One night she'd be in Ruby's bedroom, the next out in the barn with the other goats."

"Well, thanks, Mrs. Crocker."

"Stephanie, please. We're so grateful to you for all you did for Billy. We thought you'd get a kick out of our sweet baby. Oh, I hope Tom told you not to be alarmed if she faints. It's the breed. They sometimes stiffen up when they get excited. It's a genetic condition called myotonia congenita. They might freeze or topple over, but it only lasts twenty or thirty seconds. Doesn't hurt 'em, just looks scary."

"Thanks for telling me. Honestly, I'm not sure I can keep her, but I'll give it a try."

"That's the spirit. You take care, Ms. Jeffers."

Greta rung off and shook her head, strolling to the kitchen window to check on Daisy. When she couldn't see her, she headed for the back door, only to find the little goat waiting on the doorstep.

"Okay, you little devil," she said, opening the door. Daisy pranced in on hooves clicking on the tile floor.

I must be insane, Greta thought, grabbing her phone and calling her friend, Pam Morgan Rodriguez. After she related the goat story and her afternoon with Murph, the friends decided to meet for dinner at Bluewater Seafood, a popular restaurant down the coast south of their village of Horseshoe Crab Cove.

CHAPTER 3

"This has been the most incredible day," Greta said as the friends met and were ushered to a table at Bluewater Seafood. "Wow, how'd we get this table?"

Pam smiled, nodding to the waiter. "You forget who I'm married to." Her husband knew every restaurant owner within fifty miles.

Katie, the waitress, appeared with menus and took their drink orders. "Two chardonnays and waters, gotcha."

Pam leaned forward, grinning. "Of course, I want to hear about your new pet, but first tell me about cute Murphy O'Neill. Sounds like you had a fun day."

"Cute doesn't begin to describe the man. He's gorgeous, and what a nice guy. I mean, he spent the whole day helping me catch Daisy, clean out the shed, and get her settled. He even went to town to pick up a load from Cove Feed and Grain. I mean, who does that for someone he barely knows?"

"Obviously someone who wants to know you better."

"Have you forgotten his girlfriend?"

"You mean Sadie?"

Greta nodded. "Yes, lithe, lovely Sadie."

"Who he broke up with six months ago?"

"Really?"

"Really."

"Here you go, ladies," Katie said as she returned and set down their drinks. "Can I tell you the specials?"

"Please," Pam said, gazing up at her. Her friend possessed an ethereal beauty that, at the same time, came across as wholesome and down-to-earth. Her strawberry-blonde hair fell to her shoulders, and her lovely face was splayed with freckles.

They both ordered specials, Greta the halibut, Pam the bluefish. When Katie disappeared, Greta leaned forward. "So he's not with Sadie anymore?"

Pam smiled. "Nope."

"What about someone else?"

"Nope, or not that he's told his best friend, and they've been together a lot lately planning Field and Fire."

"So, if a girl were interested...?"

"You never know."

"Well, actually, he invited me to go to Sandy's tonight. Wanna come? I'm sure not walking in there alone."

"Sure. Let's do it. Maybe I can get Sandy to join us, although he pretty much steers clear of the place."

"Where is he tonight?"

"With Maisie," Pam said, referring to her husband's daughter from his first marriage to Lolly Rogers. "But her mom wants her back after supper."

"I dunno. There's also Daisy to contend with. No telling what's she's gotten into while I'm away."

"Where did you leave her?"

"In the shed. I felt so guilty. We'll only stay at Sandy's a short time."

Over dinner, they chatted about life and work. When Pam first moved down from Maine, she had worked with Greta at the high school, so her friend caught her up on all the gossip there. They also chatted about Sandy's plans for Field and Fire. After Katie cleared their dinner dishes, they declined dessert or coffee and headed out. They had come in two cars, so Pam followed Greta to the club, which was hopping, not an empty space in the lot. They parked a quarter mile up the Coast Road and walked down. As they neared the club, a familiar truck came up alongside them. Pam's handsome husband called, "Want a lift?"

They waved him off. "Watch this," Pam said as he backed up and parked behind Murph's truck. "Why didn't we think of that?"

"'Cause we're not Sandy," Greta said, laughing as they climbed the front steps, music deafening now, Mitch Corcoran's deep throaty voice belting out a song.

"If you got anything to say to me, better do it now," Pam cried. "'Cause I won't hear a thing in there."

Greta told the guy at the door that Murph had comped them, and he stood aside. "Come on in, ladies. You're always free anyway, Ms. Rodriguez," he added, nodding to Pam.

"Let's wait for Sandy over here," Pam shouted, and they made their way along the south wall that held rows of hooks for coats and jackets.

Suddenly Greta felt a warm hand on her shoulder. "Hey, you made it."

She smiled. His touch was electric. "Hi."

He turned his hundred-watt smile from her to her companion. "Hey, Pam, is Sandy coming?"

"Right behind you, buddy," a voice said as Pam's dark-haired husband appeared at her side. "And my truck's behind yours out back." He leaned over to kiss his wife's cheek. "Hey, babe."

Sandy's coal-black eyes danced with light. He had a body to die for and gave off the kind of smoldering heat that made women swoon. From the moment she'd met him years earlier, Greta had always thought of Sandy Rodriguez as the most gorgeous man in town. Tonight, his former club manager was right up there. She already liked to think of him as *my Murph*.

"Where do you feel like sitting?" Murph asked. "Just tell me, and I'll make it happen."

"Ladies?" Sandy said.

"The deck," they said in unison.

"Deck it is. What can I get you to drink?"

Both women asked for seltzer, and the two men headed for the bar with promises to meet them on the deck. Greta and Pam fought their way across the dance floor to the double doors open to the ocean breezes. Miraculously, they found an empty table and grabbed it.

"Here you go," Murph said, handing them both their drinks. "Your hubby got waylaid," he said to Pam. "He'll be right out."

"Busy night," Pam said, smiling up at him.

"Yup, 'fraid I've gotta get back in, but if I get free, maybe we can grab one dance?" he said, looking at Greta.

She blushed. "Sure, of course."

"Okay, then."

As he disappeared, Pam gave her a look. "Now that's a man who knows what he wants, and he wants you!"

"Ha-ha. He is pretty cute, though, and it's certainly been a while since I've had someone in my life, especially a nice guy like Murph. I don't count lecherous, narcissistic Hugh Cochran."

"He was kind of a loser. I'm surprised the chemistry department and the administration tolerates his behavior toward women students. In the short time I was there, I fielded several complaints from both sexes."

Greta sipped her drink, nodding at her friend. "I know. Unfortunately he's hard to get rid of. He's one of the high school's four PhDs, he's respected in his field, and there's a huge shortage of science teachers."

"What about encouraging women scientists? I would think he's scared away a number of them?"

"Let's not talk about that lecher. I'm afraid your husband has been swallowed up by his many fans," Greta said.

"Always happens, which is why he steers clear of this place most of the time. Customers run up and complain about Cady's changes, and his former employees all want to grumble too."

"Well, here he comes, looking like a gorgeous swashbuckler, and with his first mate too," Greta said as Sandy and Murph stepped onto the deck.

"Sweetheart, they're playing our song," Sandy said, gazing down at Pam.

Murph came around to stand beside Greta. "How 'bout it?" he asked, smiling as he extended his hand to her.

"Love to," she said, taking his hand and standing on wobbly legs. Just his touch was enough to make her go weak in the knees.

They walked hand in hand to the dance floor as strains of Dolly Parton's "I Will Always Love You" began. "Oh, I love this song," Greta said as he pulled her into his arms.

"Me too," he said, his breath warm and sexy, lips brushing against her ear as he pulled her closer.

Greta stiffened in surprise.

"Too much?" he asked, gazing down at her.

She smiled. "It's been a while, but no. Just right," she said, resting her head on his wide, strong chest, relaxing against him.

"Good," he whispered.

CHAPTER 4

After an intense, heart-stopping dance, Murph had been pulled away for work, and Greta, Pam, and Sandy departed soon afterward. Once home, Greta headed out to the shed to check on Daisy, where loud plaintive bleating greeted her. So inside she came to sleep on the rug beside her mistress's bed. *How could my dull, predictable life be so turned upside down in just twenty-four hours?* Greta thought as she drifted off to sleep.

The next morning was Sunday, so she headed into town for Meeting for Worship. A birthright Quaker, Greta seldom missed services in the small clapboard-sided meetinghouse in Southport. Her parents, along with a handful of others, had started the meeting shortly after moving to the area, and the tiny church continued to have a small but committed congregation. Greta happily served on the board and also several committees, including hospitality. The hospitality crew served refreshments after services each week. To this end, she stopped at the Moon and Stars, the excellent local bakery, for muffins and pastries on her way through town.

As Greta hopped out of her car, she heard, "Morning, sweetie," behind her. Frankie Brown, a tall, sixty-something with curly salt-and-pepper hair and piercing blue eyes, greeted her at the door. Beside her stood Frankie's dear friend, Helen Winthrop. The two women usually served as the official greeters, and today was no exception. Greta chatted with them, then headed to the basement common room and kitchen to help set up.

Finally seated, she breathed a contented sigh, grateful to be in the sacred place where she felt connected to her beloved parents and the worshippers around her. After the clerk opened the meeting, silence prevailed for most of the hour. A few people felt moved to speak, and then the clerk, Belle Pollart, rose to close the meeting with Lucille Clifton's poem, "mulberry fields." A strong, imposing figure, Belle's cropped salt-and-pepper hair framed a lovely oval face, her dark skin flawless. Belle's deep voice boomed in the silent meetinghouse. Greta closed her eyes, taking in the images the poem evoked and feeling enormously blessed to be in the presence of so many kindred spirits, including Belle, who had provided her such solace over the last year.

Calm and peaceful, she emerged from the meetinghouse an hour later, the warm sun on her face. She decided to take each day as it unfolded in regard to her new house pet *and* handsome Murphy O'Neill, who had left her breathless and on fire after their dance the previous evening. *What will Daisy have gotten into while I've been gone?* she mused, heading up the Coast Road.

Greta found the little goat resting in the shade in the backyard. When she stepped onto the terrace, the kid hopped up and came to her side. "Hey, Daisy! How are you doing?" She crouched down to pet the fluffy animal.

After considering her options, which included garden chores, writing up case reports, and house cleaning, she chose gardening. She spent the afternoon weeding, raking, and cleaning out garden beds, Daisy at her heels most of the time. As she hauled the last load of clippings to the compost pile, her cell phone rang. Greta had placed the phone on a bench, and the sound attracted Daisy, who ran toward the bench. She raced to overtake her, afraid the goat might decide the phone was a snack. *Goats eat everything, right?*

Snatching up the phone, she said, "Hello?"

"Hey, it's Murph. How're you doing?"

She loved the sound of his voice. "Great. Just spent three hours in the backyard with my helper at my heels."

"How's she settling in?"

"Pretty good. She's definitely a house goat, though, at least at night."

"Uh-oh."

Greta laughed. "It's fine, and she's good company."

"Hey, listen, I'm sorry I had to disappear last night. I looked for you for another dance, but you guys had vanished."

"You seemed pretty busy."

"Yeah, Saturdays are the worst. I was... I mean, if you're not too busy... I was... well I was thinking we might grab dinner this week? The club's closed Monday and Tuesday nights, but I can usually get someone to open on another night, if that's better for you?"

"Tuesday would work. I only work a half day Wednesday because it's my report writing day and I usually stay home in the morning." *Too much information! You are babbling!*

"Tuesday would be great. Around six thirty? I can pick you up."

"Perfect."

"What do you like? We could go seafood at Bluewater or the Grille. There's always Buster's if you feel like burgers, or Ballard's if you want fancy. You choose."

"You know, I haven't been to Buster's or had a great burger for a while. Let's go there."

"You got it. See you Tuesday, then?"

"Yes," she said, then hung up, a huge smile on her face.

CHAPTER 5

Monday morning was always busy for Greta. Behavior issues left over from the weekend skirmishes meant she was called into classrooms more than usual. During the little downtime she had, she completed reports and scheduled meetings for the week. As she went about each task, dinner with Murph never left her mind. No man had ever had this effect on her. *Ever.* Just the thought of him sent shivers and waves of heat through her body. Just before lunch, she wrote Murphy O'Neill instead of her student's name on a report. *Down, girl*, she thought, shaking herself. *You're getting way ahead of yourself! It was one dance, and we're going out for burgers.*

After correcting her mistake, she saved the document and headed to the teacher's lounge for lunch. She went back and forth as to where she ate lunch, sometimes in her office, sometimes with her colleagues, but she needed the distraction of others today. She was also hoping to catch Pete Sanders, one of the PE teachers, to debrief about a student he'd sent to her first period. As she grabbed her canvas lunch bag from the fridge, Hugh Koffman came up behind her.

"I hear you're a farmer now," he said.

Greta looked up at his smirking face. *How could I ever have thought*

he was handsome? He's nothing but a patronizing, self-absorbed buffoon!
"Word travels fast."

"I ran into Tom Crocker at Averill's," he said, referring to the town's general store.

"And my goat was the topic of your conversation?"

"No, I actually overheard Tom telling Hank about him."

"It's a her, actually." Greta turned away and sat at the far end of the table next to several colleagues, hoping to forestall any further conversation with Hugh.

No such luck. He plunked himself across from her, opened up his lunch, a gigantic Italian grinder, and grinned. "Are you gonna keep her?"

"Not sure."

"Keep who?" asked Peggy Latham, chair of the English department.

"Greta's got a goat. Didn't she tell you?" Hugh said.

"Well, since I just got her this weekend and this is the first time I've seen Peggy today, we haven't had time to catch up."

Greta turned to Peggy and briefly filled her in about Daisy before changing the subject to talk about a student. Fortunately, the table filled, and Hugh's attention was diverted for the rest of the meal.

"Hey, this is really coming along," Murph said as he and Sandy walked through the newly constructed restaurant. Perched on the bluffs, the structure featured enormous windows on all sides. The entire east wall was glass, affording spectacular views of the river. Murph whistled as they stood side by side gazing out at the river. "Sandy's has nothing on this, buddy."

"It is pretty cool, isn't it?" his friend said. "We're hoping for a soft opening in six weeks."

"You're kidding? That soon?"

"The finish guys think they can have things pretty well along in a week, then all the appliances and kitchen will go in. Everything's been measured and ordered. Sam Morgan's plans are really specific, so that part was relatively easy." Sam Morgan, nephew of Sandy's father-in-law, Richard Morgan, was the architect for the project and had flown up from Maryland a number of times to supervise.

The two sat at a table near the east windows, still partially covered with brown paper. Sandy gave him a look. "So, it's decision time, buddy. Are you onboard, or do I start looking for a manager? I mean, I'll be here and the chef runs the kitchen, but we need someone for day to day management. That person will also be liaising with the winery."

"You know my loyalty is with you," Murph said. "Always. But Elizabeth hasn't hired anyone to replace me. As far as I can tell, she's been dragging her heels. I can talk to her. I didn't realize you'd be opening so soon."

"This your decision, Murph? Be straight with me and yourself. If you'd rather stay with the club, I totally support you."

"Honestly, it's not the same over there. I think I want out, but let me talk to Elizabeth."

"I need you yesterday, my friend."

"I know. Can I have till the end of the week?"

"Take two weeks, but then I'll have to start looking."

"Thanks," Murph said, running his fingers through his hair.

"As I told you before, I'll match Cady's salary or more. Hours will be slightly different."

"No prob," Murph said, standing. "Gotta book it. Orders coming in this afternoon."

When she got home from school, Greta found Daisy curled in her favorite spot under a Japanese maple. The shed door was propped open, and she could see the little kid had upset the water trough and pulled hay all over the place. She grabbed some carrots and celery from the fridge and headed out to greet her. "Hey, you," she called from the terrace, and Daisy came running.

Greta sat on the grass, and the little goat curled up on her lap, licking her face. "Here you go, baby," she said, offering a carrot, which she gobbled up. She loved the celery too. After her snack, she scampered around the lawn for several minutes, then paused as if frozen. As she watched, Daisy stood stiff and still for twenty seconds then toppled over on the grass. Greta jumped up and ran to her side, but Daisy was already moving about, and soon after, she leapt to her feet, hooves pawing the ground.

"You gave me a fright, Daisy Belle," Greta said, ruffling her fur. She decided she would ask Tom Crocker for a good reference guide on goats and also resolved to google for information about Tennessee fainting goats.

CHAPTER 6

Tuesday night, Greta took care to select casual clothes that made her feel sexy and attractive. She wore sage-green skinny jeans, a white T-shirt, and a simple jewel-neck, bolero-style cardigan, its fern motif matching the color of her jeans. The soft texture of the silk-blend fabric and three-quarter bell sleeves made her feel cool and comfortable. She slipped on leather flip-flops and silver-and-sea-glass earrings. As she ran a brush through her short hair, the front doorbell rang. She glanced at her bedside clock. *Six thirty on the dot.*

"Wow, you look sensational," Murph said when she opened the door.

Greta smiled, knowing her cheeks were now bright red. Gracefully accepting compliments had never been her forte. "Thanks," she sputtered.

In jeans and sneakers, Murph wore a collared short-sleeve dress shirt, the checkered pattern the colors of the sea. He looked good enough to eat. As they stood in the doorway, Daisy broke the ice by skittering up to greet him.

"Hey, little lady," he said, stooping to scoop her up in his arms. "What're you doing in here?"

"She's definitely a house goat," Greta said. "Apparently, she's been living inside at the Crockers', so I doubt she'll happy in the shed at night. I do put her out there when I go out, though, so bring her along."

"Why? You afraid she'll trash the house?"

"Maybe. I'm taking no chances."

He grinned, following her through the house and out the terrace door. "Sounds like Daisy's a keeper."

"Maybe. I'm giving us a week together, then I'll decide." Greta grabbed a banana and some carrots from the table and headed for the shed. "She's actually a great little companion and super good. The Crockers also trained all their goats to do their business in one spot instead of all over the yard. Stephanie called to explain. Daisy has already found her litter box behind the shed. The only thing is the fainting, which is a little scary."

"Does she do it a lot?"

"Not so far. Just once, at least that I've observed. Okay, set her down." Greta tossed the treats onto the floor of the shed. "Let's go. I leave the door open for her to come in and out."

As Daisy enjoyed her treats, they hurried across the lawn and into the house. Greta grabbed her bag. "Ready?"

"All set," he said, opening the door for her.

As she brushed past, his woodsy scent mixed with ginger and citrus surrounded her, and Greta felt faint. *Could the man be any more irresistible?*

BUSTER'S WAS RELATIVELY QUIET ON A WEEKNIGHT, SO THEY FOUND A table right away in the quieter back room. The back room windows looked out on Leeside, the tiny village just southwest of Horseshoe Crab Cove. "I haven't been here in ages," Greta said, as she sat across from him at the small, brightly painted table. Each table had been painted by a local artist, each unique and different. Theirs was a riot of color, an impressionist homage to Van Gogh's flowers. The artist, Tegan Fitzgerald, a professor at nearby Clifton College, had signed the corner.

"Buster's is one of my favorites," Murph said. "But then I'm pretty lowbrow." He gazed across the table, giving her a hundred-watt smile.

"Me too, although I like to get dressed up once in a while. I suppose as a goat owner, my brow has lowered a bit."

"Well, you're miles above me."

"Have you always lived in Horseshoe Crab Cove?"

"Nope, in fact I don't live here now. I rent a place in Southport. Little more than a fisherman's shack, but it suits me fine. I grew up in Bayport, or just outside. My folks still live there on what they call their mini farm."

"So you went to Bayport schools?"

"Through ninth grade, then they shipped me off to Middlesex, where I met another wild man, Sandy Rodriguez, and, as they say, the rest is history. Been best buddies ever since."

"Did you go to college together?"

He shook his head. "Wanted to. Miraculously, we both got into Yale, but my folks wanted me closer to help with the farm, so I ended up at Clifton."

"What was your major?"

"Spanish. Believe it or not, I seem to be good at languages. I minored in environmental science and wanted to go to grad school, but Dad needed me. So enough about me. Let's hear your life history," he said as their waitress appeared.

"Hey, folks, I'm Suzie. What can I get you?" With her curly hair in a ponytail, wearing a red-and-white checkered shirt, jean shorts, and sneakers, Suzie stood pen and pad in hand, waiting.

They both ordered burgers, Greta a mushroom and gruyere burger called the Lady Gaga, and Murph, the double bacon cheeseburger with onions, aptly named the Hulk.

"You got it," Suzie said. "What about something to drink besides water?"

They ordered a pitcher of Crab IPA, made by a small craft brewery in Horseshoe Crab Cove, and Suzie disappeared.

Murph leaned forward. "Okay, your turn—let's have it."

She smiled, loving the flecks of light in his beautiful brown eyes.

"It'll be the shortest history known to man. Grew up in Newton, went to Northeastern, then got my master's in social work. I worked a couple of years in Boston, then Cove High hired me, so here I am."

"This is such a small town. Funny we never ran into each other before Sandy and Pam started dating."

"I'm a newbie. I'd only arrived about a year before Pam moved down from Maine. My last few years have been pretty wrapped up in my parents' illnesses and caregiving."

"No time for dating?"

She made a face. "Well, I did date a colleague for a while. Big mistake. He's kind of a jerk, but then maybe we just weren't compatible. Who knows?"

Suzie set down the pitcher of beer and two frosted glasses. "Here you go. Burgers will be out in ten minutes or so."

During dinner, they chatted about their day, the restaurant, Sandy's, Greta's work, and the care and feeding of Daisy. Always there was a kind of electricity in every word, every meeting of their eyes, and Greta was grateful they were in a booth with the table between them. Occasionally, their legs brushed against one another, and that was enough to raise her temperature. As Murph paid the check, she took a deep breath, trying to stay calm in thinking, *What's next?*

"Nice night for a walk," Murph said as they exited Buster's around eight thirty.

"Whatcha have in mind? I sure need some kind of exercise to walk off that huge burger and gallon of beer."

"Come on," he said, grabbing her hand. "We can walk through the village and circle back. It's about a mile. What do you say?"

"Perfect," she said, the warmth of his touch both comforting and terrifying. *I really like this man,* she thought. *Too much at this stage of the game.*

"I don't come to Leeside often," she said, fighting to stay calm and collected.

"Me neither, but it's actually a cool place. I've sometimes thought if I bought a place, it'd be here. I couldn't afford anything on the coast, and prices in Horseshoe Crab Cove have skyrocketed since it's been discovered."

"The Barnum's Ledge Inn and Resort has really brought 'em in," she said, referring to a newly restored property on the harbor.

"Yup. They did a great job. Sandy's ex has already moved out there with her fiancé, Jack Faulkner. Sandy says their house is spectacular."

Greta nodded. "Where Lolly used to live was pretty spectacular too. I rented one of the cottages from Mavis when I first came to town. That's such an amazing property." Mavis LaSalle, Lolly Rogers's mother, owned Cove Inn and Spa, a beautiful estate east of town. A much-sought-after wedding and event venue, the spa was usually booked for several years in advance. There were three cottages on the estate as well as an enormous, restored mansion. A Jane Austen fan, Mavis had dubbed the inn and her home Netherfield Manor.

As they strolled, he continued to hold her hand, stroking gently with his strong, rough fingers. "Yeah, that's Horseshoe Crab Cove and this whole area really, spectacular, one-of-a-kind properties. Look at Morgan's Fire, where the new restaurant is gonna be. What a place."

"Richard Morgan had a vision, and he's living in it now. I've only been there a couple of times with Pam, but I've also been at a couple of events. Richard is really generous in sharing the farm with the village."

"Sure is."

"I'd love to see Field and Fire sometime," she said as they turned off the main street and headed down a more dimly lit lane.

"Anytime. Happy to give you a tour. Come on, this is my favorite part of the walk." He led her into a park toward a long, covered arbor that stood at its center. The two-hundred-foot-long arbor was lit with tiny twinkle lights.

Greta felt like she was entering a magical, undiscovered land. "I've never seen this before."

"Cool, huh?"

"I'll say," she whispered as they stepped through the entrance.

THERE WAS A POINT MIDWAY THROUGH THE ARBOR WHERE ALL LIGHT was obliterated and they walked in total darkness. The realization made Greta gasp. Here she was with a man she barely knew in a strange place, far from anything familiar. She shivered. Murph touched her hand, then his arm circled her shoulders. "Hey, you okay?"

"It's really dark in here, isn't it?"

"I got you, babe. We'll see light soon."

"It's like we're in a cocoon."

He chuckled, his woodsy scent comforting. They hadn't known each other long, but she did know this man. Knew she could trust him and that he'd protect her no matter what. She leaned her head on his shoulder.

"Know what I'd like to do right now?" he asked, his voice husky.

"I have a pretty good idea," she said, turning to face him, her arms circling his broad shoulders.

He had no trouble finding her lips in the inky blackness, capturing them in a deep kiss, his tongue circling hers as she responded. Her body warmed from head to toe and Greta let out a deep sigh, relaxing into the comfort of his strong arms now holding her close. As the kiss deepened, she felt his arousal against her stomach. *Wow, this man is hot!*

Murph's hands caressed, finding her breasts, massaging and teasing until her nipples stood hard like ripe buds. "You are so beautiful," he murmured.

"Where's this going?" she asked, breathless and panting.

"Where do you want it to go?" he growled, his lips tracing a delicious trail down her neck.

Breathless, she whispered, "I know what my answer would be at home, in familiar surroundings, but here in this strange place in the pitch dark, I'm just a bit out of my element."

"You could have fooled me, babe." He slid his hands under her T-shirt and moved up to cup each breast as he kissed her again.

Greta began a slow rhythmic rubbing against him, her body on fire as his erection sent waves of pleasure through her. "This is nice," she murmured.

"It'd be even nicer if you'd lose those jeans."

"Help me, then," she said, kissing his neck, her hands tracing the lines of his chest.

"Gladly." He deftly unzipped her and slipped both jeans and panties down her legs, kicking them aside as his fingers moved between her thighs, parting her legs and moving upward. "There you are," he said, smiling as he found her clit, and Greta moaned in pleasure. It didn't take long for him to bring her straight to the moon and back.

Her orgasm left her weak-kneed and panting. As she recovered, she clasped the top button of his jeans and whispered, "You turn now," as she unzipped and released him.

"Wow, are you ever a surprise," Murph said as he reached down and retrieved a condom from his wallet. After slipping it on, he lifted her to straddle him. "You got an amazing ass. Tell me, is this too much?"

"Not enough," she said, rearing back and guiding him into her.

"Oh, babe," Murph groaned as their frenzied lovemaking began, Greta above him, holding on for dear life, matching his every thrust as they traveled to an explosive, simultaneous climax.

He whispered, "Now my legs are shaking, but don't worry, I won't drop you."

Greta leaned her head against his shoulder. "I'm not worried," she said softly, "but we probably ought to keep going. I can actually see a tiny bit of light at the end of the tunnel."

He kissed her neck, then her cheeks and nose. "This was beyond incredible. Like nothing I've experienced before. Ever."

"Me either," she said, kissing him gently.

"Okay, then," he said, groaning as he lifted her and withdrew from her warmth. After setting her on the ground, he kissed her forehead, then stooped to help her retrieve her clothing.

When they were fully dressed, they walked arm in arm to the far end of the arbor. As they emerged, Murph's truck was visible at the edge of the park, and they headed to it.

"I don't want tonight to end," she said. "But work tomorrow. Early meetings."

"Me too."

When they arrived at the cottage, Murph helped her bring Daisy in for the night.

Every fiber of her being wanted to drag him into her bedroom and ask for a repeat of their lovemaking, but instead, she walked him to the truck. "I had a wonderful time. Thanks."

"Can we do this again soon?"

"I'd like that."

"Night, Greta," he said. One last kiss, then he hopped into the truck.

"Night."

She stood on her steps, silhouetted in the light, and Murph thought he'd never seen anything more beautiful or frightening in his life.

CHAPTER 7

"Heard you had a hot date last night, buddy," Sandy Rodriguez said as Murph slid into the booth across from him. They had met at the Brickyard Diner, a little hole-in-the-wall eatery halfway between Horseshoe Crab and Bayport. They often met there for the incredible breakfasts, but also to get out of town when they didn't want to be interrupted.

"It was hot, all right, and it's totally freaked me out. I mean, the woman's amazing."

"So what's the problem?" Sandy knew his friend's difficult history with women and his past, but always hoped the next woman would change all that.

"You know me. Can't commit, and Greta Jeffers is a keeper. I'll muck it up and end up hurting her, and I just don't want to be that shithead."

"You aren't that shithead. This time could be different. Just take it slow. Keep it casual and friendly and see where it goes."

"Too late for that," Murph said, his cheeks reddening. "And that's all I'm gonna say about that."

"Well, my advice—not that I'm an expert—would be to give it a chance. Go out a few more times, see how you're feeling then."

Murph shrugged. "Maybe."

The waitress appeared, and they both ordered the Brickyard special, two eggs, locally cured bacon, and some of the best hash browns anywhere. As she disappeared, Sandy turned to him. "So what's it gonna be?"

"I'm in," Murph said. "Elizabeth's coming by sometime in the next few days, and I'm gonna tell her. I'll give her three weeks' notice with an offer to consult occasionally if it doesn't interfere with my work at Field and Fire."

"You've just made my day, Murphy O'Neill." Sandy extended his hand across the table, and his friend took it. "Didn't know how I was gonna do it without you."

The friends spent breakfast talking about the next few weeks. Sandy asked him to take over all ordering oversight and to collaborate with the newly hired chef, Meryl Stockdale. They had found Meryl through her much older brother Johnny, who cooked for the Arizona Morgans at their camp for handicapped children, Emma's Dream. Johnny had been one of the West Coast's foremost chefs, but, semiretired now, he only took on "love projects" like the camp. Brother and sister had run several restaurants together, and most recently, Meryl had spent several years living and working in Italy. She'd returned to the States hoping to find a position as executive chef at the right restaurant. When Sandy Rodriguez called, she was pretty sure she'd found it. Her visit a month earlier convinced her.

"Meryl gets in Monday," Sandy continued as he paid the check. "Looking forward to you two getting up to speed. We're scouting places for her to live right now. Richard and Lucy have offered the farmhouse, and they certainly have plenty of space, but I'm sure she'd like to get settled somewhere of her own."

"I can help with that, if you like," Murph said as they walked out into the bright sunlight.

"Pam and her sister Gail have been on it, my mom too, but I'll let them know you're available."

"Gonna be fun," Murph said.

Sandy grinned. "We have high expectations. The connection with the winery alone is going to put us on the map, or so my father-in-law thinks."

"The Wolfman's gonna do great things," Murph said, referring to the winery manager, Wolfie Morgan, Richard Morgan's youngest and Sandy's brother-in-law.

"You sound like his dad. Actually, Wolfie does have something about him. People are drawn to him, and the PR his sister Gail has put out featuring him has gotten great reviews.

The two friends parted in the diner lot. "I'll let you know how it goes with Elizabeth," Murph said.

"Great," Sandy said, hopping into his truck. "And good luck with your lady love."

"Ha-ha," Murphy said, waving as his boss drove away. *I can think of a thousand and one ways I'll screw this one up.*

Since her Sunday was free, Greta decided to take Daisy out to the Crockers for a visit with her sisters and brothers. She called and Stephanie said, "Sure come on out. We'd love to see you both."

They arranged for Greta and Daisy to come around two and she hung up, deciding to spend the morning on housework. Pangs of sadness washed over her as she moved through each room. It was times like this when she most regretted being an only child. She had no sisters or brothers to lean on, to call for a chat. Her closest friend, Keira Abbott, lived in Southport, but frequently traveled in her job as an attorney specializing in environmental law. Greta had become friendly with Pam Morgan Rodriguez and sometimes socialized with colleagues from the high school, but in truth, she was a bit of a loner. Her mother had often called Greta her little hermit since her daughter had spent so much time alone as a child. The truth was, Greta wasn't a joiner and had declined playing most team sports except tennis.

Shake it off, she told herself as she hauled out the vacuum. *Wallowing never helped anyone.*

CHAPTER 8

"Welcome, welcome!" Stephanie Crocker called, waving from their back porch as Greta untied Daisy and lifted her from the truck. The Crockers' farm was just "off peninsula," lying northwest of the village of Horseshoe Crab Cove. A small operation in comparison to the huge properties of Richard Morgan's Fire and the Miller's Land's End, the Crockers raised goats, sheep, and alpacas, as well as a flock of exotic and local chickens. They sold the wool from the goats, sheep, and alpacas, and the chicken eggs of varying hues. Their eggs were highly sought after by local restaurants as well as towns and cities as far away as Boston. The Crockers also had a small but growing artisan cheese company using their goats' milk and cows' milk from a local dairy.

No one needed to direct Daisy. As soon as Greta unleashed her, she took off to the goat pen, bleating all the way. "Oh, what a sweetie she is," Stephanie said, smiling as they watched the other goats run to the fence to greet her. "Come on, we'll let them play, and we can visit in the shade." The tall, sturdy woman with flaxen hair and freckles led the way down the lawn. She was in jeans and a flannel shirt, the sleeves rolled to her elbows. She wore running shoes, expensive ones. When not farming, Stephanie Crocker was one of the top area runners. She specialized in ten-kilometer races and half marathons and was a familiar sight in the early morning, jogging along the village roads.

Greta gazed from the sneakers to her hostess. "Been in any races lately?"

"I wish. We've been out straight these past few weeks with a huge cheese order and all the egg deliveries. One of our hands, Lonny Polk, broke his leg. On a motorcycle," she added, frowning. "So we're a bit short-staffed. I'm actually going to call the high school and ask them to post the job in case there are a couple of strong, reliable kids looking for work."

"That's too bad about Lonny. I can certainly help get the word out."

"That'd be terrific, thanks. Honestly, I'd like to strangle Lonny. He knows better and was fooling around with his buddies. He's been working for us for almost ten years, so his absence is huge."

She opened the goat pen gate, and Daisy frolicked in, almost immediately fainting as her family crowded around her.

"Oh, boy," Stephanie said. "She's always been our little drama queen when there's any excitement."

Stricken, Greta watched her tiny pet lying in the dirt just inside the pen. "Oh, should I go to her? This is one of the things I wanted to ask you about."

Stephanie waved her hand. "No, leave her be. Nothing to worry about. This breed does it all the time. She'll be right as rain in five minutes. Come on, come sit. I have iced tea or lemonade."

After observing Daisy stirring, Greta followed her host to a lovely patio created under an enormous sycamore tree. Comfortable wrought iron chairs and a table welcomed them. A tray on the table held two pitchers, glasses, and a plate of cookies. "This is so nice of you, Steph. I'm sure you have a million things to do."

"Not a bit of it. I'm delighted to take a break. Tom and I always say we shouldn't work on the Lord's day, but that's hard when you're keeping up a farm. What can I pour you?"

Greta chose half lemonade, half iced tea, and Stephanie followed suit. They then spent an enjoyable hour talking goats and life. As

Greta rose to leave, she said, "Do you think it's cruel to Daisy to keep her by herself?"

Her hostess smiled. "From what you've told me, she's not by herself."

"Well, she's alone all day while I'm at work."

"My guess is she's just fine. If it's a particularly long day, or anytime you have to be away, feel free to drop her off. One more kid's not going to make a difference, and we love to see her."

"Thanks, Stephanie," Greta said, hugging her. "I'm not sure I could handle two goats."

The other woman laughed. "Your Daisy's fine. We wouldn't have given her to you if we didn't think she'd be fine on her own. None of our other goats get the one-on-one attention she'll get from you."

"Now to corral her. She might not want to leave."

"Let's just see," Stephanie said as they unlatched the gate to the goat enclosure. Animals were everywhere, behind the three sheds, some on top of a tree house, and a couple perched on huge boulders. Greta spotted Daisy lying next to a tiny white kid. She called, "Daisy!" and was surprised to see the little goat instantly raise her head and hop up, running to her. "Oh, you sweetheart," she said, squatting to pet her, then clipping the leash to her collar.

"I think your little sweetheart already knows where her home is."

Greta looked up with tears in her eyes. "Thank you so much...you and Tom. She is such a precious gift at a time when I really need her."

"Oh, honey, we're delighted she's got a good home with you."

They walked out to Greta's truck, and she stooped to lift Daisy. "You know, you might have better luck having her ride in the cab," Stephanie said. "She loves riding shotgun, and she's a real good little passenger."

Greta opened the door and placed her on the passenger seat. Daisy immediately sat on her hind legs and looked straight ahead. "Well, I guess she is a good little passenger. Thanks for the tip and for this afternoon."

"'Twas my pleasure."

"Tell Tom and Billy hello for me."

"Will do," Stephanie said, waving as Greta backed out of the driveway.

THE AFTERNOON AT THE CROCKERS HAD TAKEN GRETA'S MIND OFF Murph, but as she made dinner, her thoughts turned to the handsome, sexy Irishman who had already stolen her heart. Daisy followed her around the kitchen as she worked. At one point, she stopped and looked at her pet. "What do you think, Daisy? Should we invite him to dinner?"

The goat gave her a quizzical look, and Greta laughed, grabbing her cell phone before she could chicken out. His phone went to voicemail, but she took a deep breath and in the most casual tone she could muster, said, "Hey, Murph, how're you doing? I'm calling... Well, I mean, I'm calling to see if... I mean, I know you're super busy with the club and restaurant, but I wondered if you'd like to come to dinner sometime this week? Any day works for me. I'll do something simple. Just you, me, and Daisy. Let me know if you're free. Hope you're having a great Sunday. Bye."

She stopped to pet the soft, tiny head. "There, Daisy, I did it!" She grabbed two carrots and set them on the floor. The kid nudged and chased them around the smooth surface for several minutes before gobbling them up.

AN HOUR LATER, HER CELL RANG. "HEY, GRETA," HE SAID. "HOW ARE you?"

"Great, thanks, and you?"

"Fine, thanks. So I got your message. Would Wednesday work?"

"Perfect. Six-ish?"

"That works for me. I can have someone open the club as long as I make an appearance and close up."

"Great."

"How was your day?"

She gave him a quick description of her visit to the Crockers, and he mentioned his meeting with Sandy, then they said good night. Greta took Daisy out for a walk, then settled in with the book she was reading. *I did it,* she mused, settling on the couch. *Now let's see where it leads.*

CHAPTER 9

Monday and Tuesday went by in a blur at work. Short one social worker, Greta's workload had doubled, and student issues cropped up in all directions. She'd already had to call the Department of Children and Families when one of her students showed signs of abuse. Then three fights had broken out, two outside after lunch and a third in a PE class. While it was Greta's job to deal with the students, she often had to enlist the help of the building's two full-time police officers to deal with dangerous, out-of-control physical behaviors. An incident a year ago had ended her friend Pam's tenure as a part-time counselor at the high school when she was knocked to the floor by a student. They had yet to replace her.

Things were quieter Wednesday, and she spent time writing reports and following up with parents and various support agencies. She left school a little after two and stopped at the Land's End farm stand for produce. She then swung by the docks, where most villagers got their seafood at the fishery's store. She chose two tuna steaks, thanking Aisha Johnson, who was behind the counter.

"No Belle today?" Greta asked as she handed the young woman her credit card. Belle Pollart and her husband, Will, ran the docks and fishery on the geographically unique peninsula and harbor that was part of Horseshoe Crab Cove. Belle, along with seven other local women in their sixties, was a Darn Yarner, a group of friends who had just celebrated forty years of friendship together. Friendship characterized by support for each other, civic responsibility and love. Greta had marveled at the eight strong women who had always seemed to her to be the heart of the town. Pam's stepmother, Lucy's mother, Helen, was a Darn Yarner, as was Sandy's mom, Rosa. The Yarners had been there for Greta during her parents' illnesses and after their passing. She could never adequately repay their kindness.

"Out on the docks. She should be back soon."

"Tell her I say hi."

At home, Daisy greeted her, prancing in a circle around her the minute she stepped out on the terrace. The kid had adjusted well to spending days in the backyard, retreating to her shed as needed for rest, shelter and food. "Oh, Daisy, I'm, so glad to see you," Greta said, coming to sit on the grass, petting the tiny goat.

Greta lay back on the grass and gazed up at the sky. It was a warm afternoon, not a cloud in sight. As a child, she had lain for hours lost in the infinite blue. Now she reveled in the stillness of her beautiful backyard and the soft fluffy creature who nestled up lying beside her. An hour later, she woke and hopped up. "Whoa, Daisy! We've got to get moving!"

Murph arrived at six fifteen. Gorgeous in a cotton plaid dress shirt and jeans, he brought a bouquet of daisies and a bottle of red wine. "These are for her," he said, gazing down at Daisy, "and the wine is for us." He handed both to Greta, hugging her.

His nearness was enough to send her temperature sky-high. She smiled, stepping back. "Thanks, they're lovely. Do you think she'd mind if I put them in water?"

"Go for it. Not sure they're the best food for goats anyway. You look really pretty, by the way."

"Thanks," she said shyly. In linen capris and a white summer blouse trimmed in eyelet, Greta had taken care with her dab of makeup. She wore turquoise earrings and a matching silver bracelet. "What can I get you to drink? I have beer, wine, seltzer, and all kinds of sodas. I bet I could even find hard liquor in my parents' booze cupboard."

"Beer's fine."

She grabbed a Sam Adams from the fridge. "Bottle or mug?"

He grinned. "Bottle's fine. I'm lowbrow, remember?"

She handed him the beer and poured a glass of his wine for herself.

"I'm not much of a wine guy, but customers love all the wines from this vineyard at the club. Sandy and Wolfie insisted we stock it."

She took a sip. "It's nice."

"From a vineyard on Long Island, if you can believe it."

They took their drinks to the terrace, and Greta brought out a small plate of cheese and crackers and a bowl of Kalamata olives. "Sit, please."

Murph gazed around. "Your yard is really great. Makes mine look like a dust bowl."

She smiled. "You're looking at years of tender loving care. My parents loved this property and added to its beauty every year."

"The plantings are incredible. I hope your little friend there doesn't destroy them."

"Me too," she said, reaching down to pet Daisy, who stood by her chair. "About four years ago, they hired Kitty Bannister to redesign the gardens. It might have been one of her first jobs out of landscaping school."

"Kitty's great," he said, referring to a local landscaper.

Somehow, the way he said it made Greta think there was history between Murph and Kitty Bannister, but she didn't probe. As she watched, he turned red, then said, "We dated briefly."

"We all have pasts." As she stood, she noticed him blanch. "Are you okay?"

He shrugged. "Fine. Old ghosts."

"Well, I'm going to start the grill for the tuna steaks. Can I get you another beer?"

"Thanks, I'm good. I'm also an expert grill master. Can I help?"

"That would be great. It's a simple light. If you get it preheating, I'll be right back."

As she stepped inside the house, Greta took a deep breath, the first she'd taken since Murph's arrival. After the passion and heat of their previous meeting, their friendly conversation felt a bit weird and stilted, but she decided that casual chatting might actually slow things down to a healthier level. Everything else was prepared. She had made a couscous salad with lots of fresh vegetables, as well as a simple arugula salad with fennel and shaved parmesan. The only thing left was to grill the tuna.

She grabbed the platter from the fridge and headed back out, where she spied Murph rolling around on the grass with Daisy, the goat pouncing on his chest.

"Grill's preheating."

"Great, thanks."

"How about a tour of the garden?" he called, holding the goat at arm's length. "I'd love to hear more about all these cool plantings. Maybe it'll inspire me to fix up my place."

"Of course," she said, setting the platter on the table. "You haven't shared anything about where you live."

"Not much to share. After I moved out of my parents' place four years ago, I'd saved more than enough with what Sandy pays me to buy a duplex at the far end of town on the road to Southport. Not much, but it's mine. I rent out half, so it pays for itself. I'm lucky to have good renters."

"I'm always hearing from people that duplexes are great investments," she said as they strolled side by side, their arms brushing against each other from time to time. Although her adrenaline was through the roof, Greta also felt comfortable with him. *I trust this man who I barely know. That's a good thing.* "So here is one of my mom's favorites. It's called a Brandywine Viburnum. Its white flowers give way in the fall to beautiful clusters of maroon berries. Maroon was Mom's favorite color."

"Cool," he said, and they walked on, circling the perimeter of the yard, admiring each shrub, tree, and flower bed. Daisy followed, but refrained from disturbing any of the plantings.

As they approached the house, he paused and faced her. "This is really nice. Thanks for having me." Before she knew what was happening, he gently grasped her shoulders and pulled her close, kissing her softly.

Predictably, the kiss deepened. As she gave herself to him, arms circling his shoulders, Greta felt her legs tremble and held on tighter. Finally, she broke away and found him grinning. "We'd better get cooking, or the tuna may go bad in the sun."

Hands on her waist now, he met her eyes, a mischievous look in his. "Would that be such a bad thing if this is the alternative?"

"No, except I spent a king's ransom on them, so they ought to get cooked."

"Really?"

"Well, maybe not that much, but you get my drift."

"I do," he said, releasing her. "Lemme have 'em, and I'll get started."

Greta breathed a sigh as she handed off the platter. *Don't know what after dinner will bring, but I can make a pretty good guess!*

CHAPTER 10

Greta and Murph chatted about day-to-day happenings as they enjoyed her simple dinner. "Everything was incredible," he said as he ate the last bite. "That salad was phenomenal."

"Couldn't be easier," she said, smiling. "I used to order it at a restaurant I stopped at for dinner, which is now closed. I mostly ate there in the fall 'cause I love pumpkin ravioli and they made their own. It was to die for. Anyway, they also served this salad. The chef refused to give me the recipe for the dressing, but after experimenting, I've been able to come pretty close. It's hard to wreck a fresh-lemon dressing."

"What was the restaurant?"

"Simon's. It's between here and Bayport. Before my parents passed, I had a condo in Bayport. I'd stop at Simon's on my way home from work and have an early dinner about once a week."

"All by yourself?"

"Usually. I'm comfortable eating out alone. Did, so much of it when I worked abroad. I actually find it relaxing, and I can really savor my food." Greta blushed, realizing she was babbling. "I mean, I like to eat with people... It's just... Well, sometimes that's not possible."

His eyes met hers, and he smiled, a warm genuine smile. "No

need to explain to me. I've eaten a lot of meals solo, but mostly at greasy-spoon joints."

She laughed. "Joints?"

"Diners, bars, little hole-in-the-wall spots."

"Joints sometimes have the best food." She stood and cleared their plates. "Would you like coffee or something else? I have tiny little flans for dessert."

"I think I'm good, thanks. A tiny little flan sounds perfect after all I just ate. Can I help?"

"No, thanks. Just relax. I'll be right back."

"Looking forward to it," he said, his look conveying more than excitement about dessert.

Oh boy, she thought, afraid she'd drop the plates with her shaking hands. *This man sends me from zero to two hundred with a raise of his eyebrow.* She hurried in, threw the plates in the sink, and grabbed the flans from the fridge. After taking a few deep, calming breaths, she headed out, finding Murph sitting on the terrace steps, petting Daisy.

She grabbed spoons from the table and came to sit beside him. "Here you go," she said, handing him a plate, the crème de caramel garnished with a dollop of whipped cream flavored with amaretto.

"Thanks," he said, his shoulder rubbing hers. "Oh my God," he groaned after taking a bite. "This is incredible."

"One of my favorite desserts, but I didn't make it. These came from the Grille. Sandy's mom makes them. I'm surprised you haven't had one of Rosa's flans before."

"I have, but she doesn't put this whipped cream on them."

"Yeah, that's me."

"You're full of surprises, aren't you?"

"I hope so…or at least a few. I'd hate to be totally predictable."

"Far from it," he said, setting his empty plate beside him. Daisy immediately headed for it and licked it clean.

Greta put her plate on the grass, and the little goat licked it as well. "Probably not good for her."

"She's fine, especially since neither of us left anything worth licking," he said, turning to her, fingers gently brushing hair from her cheek. This was followed by a long, lingering kiss.

Greta responded, her tongue finding his, hands caressing his broad chest as she sighed. Daisy suddenly hopped up, hooves pawing their legs. Greta laughed, breaking the kiss and moving back. "Daisy, that's not polite."

"Sure isn't," he said. "What'll we do about this situation? 'Cause I sure want to kiss you again."

Greta stooped to collect the dessert dishes, giving him a mischievous look. "Let me put these inside where she won't break them while you ponder that question."

"No prob," he said, rising to follow her, the goat on his heels.

Greta placed the dishes on the counter and turned to find his arms open, Daisy gazing up curiously. "This is your solution?"

He set his hands on her waist, grinning like the Cheshire Cat. "Nope. I was thinking we could bring some treats to the shed and leave her outside for a bit. It's a nice night."

"And what would we be doing?"

"Whatever you like, wherever you like," he said, pulling her closer. "Now, where are those treats?"

Greta grabbed a banana and some celery stalks and said, "Okay, lead the way, oh goat tamer."

After settling Daisy in, they closed the shed door and walked across the yard holding hands.

"You know she'll be bleating in five minutes knowing we're out here."

"So maybe we go somewhere she can't hear us," he said, sweeping her up in his arms and carrying her into the house as if she were as light as a feather.

CHAPTER 11

The slider closed behind them, and he set her down, arms wrapped around her as he found her lips for a searing kiss. Greta wondered if she'd ever breathe normally again as they inched back toward the living room sofa. Despite the heat of the moment, she thought how strange it was to be doing this in her parents' home. Then he began trailing kisses down her neck and obliterated all rational thought. *I could be on a different planet*, she thought as she gave herself to him.

"Sofa or bed?" he asked, as breathless as she was.

"I think bed," she said, smiling at him, her fingers tracing the line of his jaw.

"Works for me." He grabbed her ass, bringing her up to straddle him as he headed down the hall.

"Next door on the right," she said, fingers running through his hair as her lips found his.

As they neared the bed, he set her down. "Lovely as you look, I'd love to divest you of your clothes."

"Mmm, you would, would you?" She pulled her blouse over her head, then allowed her capris to drop to the floor. She stood in front of him barefoot, in a white lacy bra and panties.

"Beautiful," he said, bending to kiss her breasts, his hands caressing her nipples to ripe, tremulous buds of sensation.

"Your turn now, Mr. O'Neill."

"Gladly." He slipped his jeans off as she unbuttoned his shirt.

Greta gazed down to spy his fully erect cock and gasped at its size. Shyly, she moved her hands down to stroke him. "Is this okay?"

"More than okay, sweetie, but I'm not sure how long I can hold on." He eased her panties down, his fingers slipping between her legs to find her clit. "You ready for me?"

"Oh so ready!" she groaned, holding on for dear life.

Murph grabbed a condom from his jeans pocket, unwrapped it, and slipped it on. Gently, he laid her on the bed, kissing her deeply as he spread her legs, then moving downward, replacing his fingers with his tongue. Greta screamed as her orgasm overtook her. She dug her fingers into his shoulders, crying, "More, more, more!"

Murph rose up, gazing down at her. "You are incredible," he whispered as he entered her, gently at first, then more forcefully.

Greta met his every thrust, her voice breathless as she whispered, "Deeper, deeper."

Though she was amazed at his size, her body had somehow opened to fully receive him, and they fit. Hungrily, she kissed him as they moved in exquisite harmony to a white-hot climax. Afterward, they collapsed into each other's arms. Murph gently maneuvered them to lie on their sides, careful to maintain their intimate connection.

"That was amazing, babe. Like nothing I've ever experienced. I don't even have words for it."

Tears in her eyes, Greta kissed his shoulder. "Me too."

Replete and sated, they drifted off to sleep, breathing as one. A little while later, Murph woke with a start. "Uh-oh—what time is it?" He glanced at her alarm clock on the bedside table. "Damn!"

Greta opened her eyes, surprised at his tone. "What is it?"

"Last thing I want to do, believe me, but I've gotta go." He kissed her, then groaned as he pulled away from her. "Torture."

She watched as he quickly dressed, then slipped out of bed to grab her robe and followed him to the front door.

"I'm so sorry, babe. I'd like nothing better than to stay all night."

She gave him a sleepy smile. "Duty calls. I understand."

He took her in his arms, kissing her one more time. "Thanks for tonight. It was perfect."

"You're welcome," she said as he stepped out into the night and sprinted to his truck. After hopping in and starting the engine, he gave a quick wave and was gone.

As the sound of the truck faded away, she heard bleating from the backyard. "Coming, Daisy!" she called. She stepped inside, locked the front door, and headed through the house to the terrace.

Only when she was in bed again, Daisy on the floor beside her, did she wonder about Murph's abrupt departure. Yes, he had to get to work, but it felt like there was something else. Like a wall had sprung up, or a door slammed shut, his warm, gentle manner gone.

When Murph arrived at Sandy's, one of the bartenders told him Elizabeth Cady was waiting in the office. "Shit!" he muttered, hurrying behind the bar toward the back of the building, oblivious to the band, a decent one, that was in full swing, the dance floor packed.

The tall blonde awaited him, impeccably dressed as always in beige linen slacks, crisp white tee, and a jacket that matched the pants. "If you're going to ask for a meeting, the least you could do is show up for it."

"I am so sorry, Elizabeth," he said, pulling up a chair beside her. "I totally lost track of time."

"A good fuck'll do that to you."

He stared at her, wondering if she were kidding.

She grinned. "I've been around long enough to smell sex on someone, honey. And you reek of it."

Unwilling to get into a discussion of sex with his employer, he said, "Can I get you something to drink?"

She reached back and grabbed her Cosmo from the table. "I'm good. Now, what gives?"

"There's no easy way to say this, so I'll come right out with it. I'm giving my official notice. I can give you a few weeks and am happy to help train a new person, but I'm out."

"You little shit."

"You had to know this was coming. I told you my loyalty was with Sandy."

"Not with the salary I'm paying you."

"I'm sorry. You can consider how you want to phase me out, find a replacement, whatever. I assume you've been looking?"

"Get out."

"Excuse me?" He stared at her, noticing for the first time the angry lines around her eyes and on her forehead. *She isn't as beautiful as a first glance would suggest.*

"I said—get the fuck out! Now."

"Okay. I'll pack up my things tomorrow and clear out."

"No, you won't. I want your keys and all your crap out now, or I'll tell the staff to burn everything." She clapped her thin hands, red tips flashing in the light. "Chop chop! Time's wasting."

Murph looked around the room and realized there was nothing he really needed from the space that had been his second home for nearly two decades. Then, reaching into his pocket, he pulled out the restaurant keys—to the doors, bar, freezers, and storerooms—and threw them on the table. "Good luck," he said, and he meant it. Sandy's was a cool place, and he hated to see it flounder. Before she could say another word, he turned and left the room, closing the door behind him.

He went behind the bar, then into the kitchens to say goodbye to his stunned staff, then, with one last look at the writhing masses on the dance floor, he walked out the front door. He was as stunned as his coworkers and felt like he was sleepwalking as he headed to his truck.

On his way home, he called Sandy, who was a night owl like himself. "Hey," his friend said. "What's happening?"

"I'm out."

"Out where?"

"I gave my notice, and the ice princess kicked me out. Took my keys and told me not to come back."

"Kinda weird, but also the best news I've heard all day. You start on Field and Fire's payroll tomorrow, buddy. Let's talk in the morning."

Murph hung up and drove on. *What a night,* he thought. *From Mount Olympus to hell to salvation in five hours or less!*

CHAPTER 12

A week went by, and Greta heard nothing from Murph. *Nothing.* Not a phone call or text. She met Pam at Morgan's Fire Saturday morning, and they decided to take a ride. Pam called down to the barn, and her sister Weezie had two of the stable horses saddled and ready to go when they arrived. Crackers was a tall, gentle American Paint, and Sheba an equally gentle chestnut Morgan. "Hey, ladies," Weezie called as they met her behind the barn. The horses were tethered to the corral fence, nickering softly.

"Thanks, sis," Pam said. "You're a peach."

"Yes, I am," the youngest Morgan daughter said, hand on hip, her short, dark hair stuffed under a baseball cap, jeans already covered with dirt. "Although you won't hear that from Ms. Stick-up-her-ass Dr. Bloom in the barn," she whispered, rolling her eyes.

"Shush, she'll hear you," Pam said, easily swinging up into Sheba's saddle.

"Like I care," Weezie said, giving Greta a leg up.

"Thanks, Weez," she said.

Her sister gazed down at her. "Be nice. Dad says she's a great vet."

"And doesn't she tell him every chance she gets?"

Pam nudged Sheba forward. "We shouldn't be more than an hour or two."

"No prob. We don't need the horses for lessons till two."

As they headed up the rise to join the Loop Trail, an eighteen-mile path that circled the village of Horseshoe Crab Cove, Greta looked over at her friend. "What was that about?"

"Let's just say that my hotheaded sister and Dr. Bloom rarely see eye to eye about the horses' care. Then there's the guys."

"Guys?"

"Both Weezie and Kiki are consummate flirts who are often after the same men."

"Oh, dear."

"Oh, dear is right. They've been all over Coop Merrick, the village blacksmith. I think they've made plays for Murph from time to time too, so you better watch out."

"No worries there. Haven't heard from him all week."

"I think Elizabeth Cady kicking him out of the club last Saturday night shook him up a bit."

Greta gazed over at her. "Really? I didn't know. What happened?"

"Well, she was pissed that he was late for a meeting he had asked for," Pam said.

"Oh, dear, that was my fault. So just 'cause he was late, she kicked him out?"

"No. The meeting was to give his notice. He'd already let her know his time at Sandy's was temporary, but I guess she thought her charms and exorbitant salary would change his mind. Anyway, the second the words were out of his mouth about leaving, I guess she told him to get out."

They had stopped at the top of the rise behind the farm and had a wide-open view of the river below them. Greta turned to her. "That sounds a little bitchy."

Pam laughed. "Well, it's done, and that's what's important. He's completely free to devote all his time to Field and Fire. I think he just feels badly for the staff he left behind, although I think a couple are planning to jump ship as well."

"Well, I'm glad for Sandy and him." *Now, it'd be nice if he'd get in touch with me!*

"The fancy chef arrives today, five days late. My normally unflappable husband has been apoplectic."

"Sandy?"

Pam nodded. "He so wants this new venture to be successful, especially the opening. Shall we head this way?"

"Lead the way," Greta said, coaxing Crackers along the path toward the Loop Trail.

~

"SO YOU HAVEN'T TALKED TO HER ALL WEEK?" SANDY ASKED AS HE AND Murph worked side by side unpacking furniture in the main dining room. The floors were in, sanded and finished, and cleaners had gone over everything the day before.

"Nope."

"Why not?"

"'Cause it's a mistake. You know what happens when I get close to someone, and Greta... Well, let's just say we couldn't have gotten any closer."

"I imagine she must be pretty confused."

"I know, and I'm sorry about that, but this is better. A clean break."

"That's cruel, don't you think?"

"Better this way."

"You don't think she deserves an explanation?"

Murph pulled a tabletop out of a box and set it on the floor. "You know I can't go there. If you want me on tap to get this running, avoidance is the best course of action."

"If you say so, buddy," Sandy said as the front door opened. "Hey, Meryl," he called as a stranger with short, stylishly cut sandy hair, a round face, and arresting blue eyes stepped in.

Murph guessed her to be in her early forties. *The famous chef has arrived, better late than never,* he thought, standing and following his boss to meet her. She was dressed in jeans and a leather jacket, clogs on her feet and a brightly colored scarf around her neck. Not what he'd call pretty, but there was something compelling about her, an intensity that radiated from those unusual eyes.

"Hey, this is my manager, Murph O'Neill. You two'll be working closely together," Sandy said, stepping aside to allow Murph space to say hello.

"Pleased to meet you, Ms. Stockdale." He extended his hand, which she grasped in a firm handshake.

"Meryl, please. Lovely to be here, albeit later than expected. I had a funeral on Wednesday."

"Oh, sorry to hear that," Murph said.

"A favorite great uncle. He was ninety-eight and lived a full, rich life. He didn't suffer, which was a comfort." She turned to Sandy. "All my things are in the car, and a mover will come next week. Any luck finding me a place?"

"Actually, yes," Sandy said. "My wife, Pam, used to rent a cool house right on the river. We thought they'd rerented it, but Pam bumped into the Fergusons, the owners, last week, and their renters fell through. It's yours if you want it."

"Sounds perfect."

"It comes fully furnished, but if you have all your own stuff, I'm sure they'd be happy to accommodate. My father-in-law, Richard, offered to store their things or yours in one of his barns."

Meryl smiled. "I travel light, so it sounds perfect. I was dreading furniture shopping. Your father-in-law, Richard, is a legend in the business world. Can't wait to meet him. Is all this property his?"

Sandy nodded. "All five hundred plus acres, although he's deeded Pam and me two acres for the restaurant. He's also a silent partner."

"Oh?"

"He knows the meaning of the word silent. Once he's confident in his people, he's a pretty hands-off guy. He likes to know what's going on and is always ready to lend support, but he rarely interferes in the running of any of the Morgan Enterprises operations, including the farm, winery, and now Field and Fire."

"Sounds like a mythic figure," Meryl said, smiling at the two friends.

Murph laughed. "You wait. There aren't many people like Richard Morgan in this world."

Sandy nodded. "Except maybe his brother, Ben, in Arizona and his college buddy Spark Foster."

"I met both of them on my brief visit to the States last summer, when I spent four days with my brother, Johnny, at Emma's Dream. I came away in love with them both."

"They don't call 'em the silver foxes for nothing."

"Too bad Ben's happily married and Spark Foster has a girlfriend. From back here, I understand."

"Helen is just a friend," Sandy said, referring to Helen Winthrop, mother of Lucy Morgan, Richard's wife.

"Sandy tells me you've been in Italy for the past several years," Murph said.

"Almost two and a half years. Loved every minute, but it was time to come home."

"Does that mean the Field and Fire menu will feature lots of Italian dishes?" Murph asked.

"That's to be determined by you all," she said, gazing from one to the other. "I'm open to anything. What I took away from my time in Italy is the enormous difference locally sourced food makes. When my brother mentioned you were looking for a farm-to-table chef, I was so excited."

"No regrets that you're not in the big city?"

"Not at all with the salary you're paying me. Besides, if we're a success, the big city will find us. The foodie community never minds traveling for spectacular food. You have PR out on food blogs and reviewers lined up, right?"

Sandy laughed. "That's the plan. My sister-in-law Gail handles PR for the farm and winery and she's got a strategy worked out for Field and Fire. Let Murph show you the kitchens and I'll call the Fergusons, see if you can have a look at the cottage."

"This way," Murph said, gesturing toward the double doors at the far end of the room. As they walked side by side, he suddenly thought of Greta and how much fun it would be telling her how the restaurant was coming along, the arrival of Ms. Super Chef and so much more. He even felt sad thinking of Daisy. *Who misses a goat?*

CHAPTER 13

Weeks went by with no word from Murph. Greta texted him a few times and always received terse replies claiming he was out straight with getting Field and Fire ready to open. The last weeks of school were busy, and she saw little of Pam, but when the friends got together Pam assured her that Murph was telling the truth. "I've barely seen Sandy since marvelous Meryl arrived," Pam said at breakfast one morning. "If they aren't working on the physical prep, Meryl, Murph, and my husband are planning menus, food orders, whatever. I offered to help, but I might as well be invisible."

Greta set her bagel down and gazed over at her friend. "I thought this was your and Sandy's baby?"

"It started out that way, but I've been out straight with clients, and the garden's gearing up for the summer. I've stepped back from the restaurant except doing the plants and flowers. That's my baby, at least for foreseeable future. Kitty Bannister helped me plan the plants for the space, and I'll come in with the fresh flowers every day."

"That's a lot of work."

Pam nodded. "Now you tell me. You should see what they want for opening night. Wanna help?"

Greta sipped her tea, not replying for a minute. "Well...you know I'd love to, but do you think it would be awkward?"

"Absolutely not! You're my friend. I've asked you. Murph will just have to deal!"

"Okay, well then, count me in."

"And you are on the guest list for opening night."

"Now *that* would be awkward, walking in all by myself."

Pam smiled, a mischievous twinkle in her eye. "I have a plan for that. My brother Ben will be home, and he already said he'd love to take you."

Greta had only met Ben Morgan, Pam's brother, once, but it had been memorable. Like all the Morgan's he was gorgeous—tall, slender with dark hair and green eyes. They met at the dedication of Laura's Community Garden on a beautiful sunny day that found an attractive blonde stranger draped on Ben Morgan's arm. The community garden was Pam's brainchild, created in memory of her mother, Laura. Townspeople tended their own plots of vegetables, herbs and flowers in a beautiful open space just off Main Street. The original plot had expanded and now encompassed four acres.

"What about his gorgeous girlfriend?"

Pam waved her hand dismissively. "Sondra? She's long gone, thank God. What a bitch, excuse my language. He may be dating someone now, who knows, but he's coming home alone and already said he'd love to take you. He remembers you."

"He does?"

"Uh-huh," Pam said, a huge grin on her lovely face.

"Ha-ha."

"I'm not kidding. You are very memorable, you know."

"Not to some people. Listen, I've gotta go. I'm meeting Tom Crocker at the farm. They've agreed to take Daisy when I'm away." She referred to her hastily arranged trip to California to visit her Aunt Sarah, her mother's sister.

"That's right. When are you leaving?"

"The day after Field and Fire's opening, as a matter of fact. It'll be good to get out of town for a few weeks."

The friends paid their check and strolled out of the Café and down Main Street, parting at the hardware store where both had parked.

"Don't give up on Murph yet. He really has been busy, and he's a complicated guy."

"I wouldn't know."

Pam squeezed Greta's arm. "What I mean is, I think he's worth hanging in to see where things go."

"Maybe, Pollyanna. Time will tell. Have a great day!" Greta hopped in her truck and headed for the Crockers'.

Murph waved to Gene and Lana LaFlamme, his renters as he mowed the lawn. "Hey, guys," he called, cutting the motor. "Sorry I've neglected this for too many weeks. I've been working twenty-four seven."

"No problem!" Gene called. "If you get stuck again, let me know. Happy to run the mower over it. Good exercise."

"Thanks, I will."

"We're looking forward to opening night!" Lana called. "How's it coming?"

"Gonna be cool," Murph said. "If we manage to pull it all together."

The LaFlammes waved and headed to their car, leaving him to his own thoughts, which, when he wasn't obsessing about work, always centered on one thing—Greta. He missed her like crazy, and it only got worse each day. He'd spied her from a distance as he drove through town, but other than that, he hadn't laid eyes on her in close to a month. *Since the night Elizabeth kicked me out.* He touched his cell phone in his back pocket, then thought, *You've done it again. What would I even say at this point?*

CHAPTER 14

Finally, the opening-night week of Field and Fire was upon them, and Morgan's Fire buzzed with activity. New signage went up, fields were mowed, and garden beds and shrubbery were weeded and trimmed. Kitty Bannister had done a spectacular job with the landscaping, and shrubs, bushes and flowers looked like they'd been there forever. Richard Morgan had donated truckloads of sod, so the lawns were green and perfect.

Wednesday morning, Greta parked at Pam and Sandy's, and they drove together to Field and Fire, parking in the winery lot adjacent to the much larger restaurant lot behind one of the barns. A walkway had been created for guests to stroll the short distance from parking lot to restaurant. There were a dozen handicap parking spots on the north side of the restaurant as well. Future plans included covering the walkway and bringing in a fleet of golf carts to shuttle diners back and forth.

"They've thought of everything, haven't they?" Greta said, marveling at the transformation of the site. As they waved to the nursery truck driver, who had just pulled up near the front door, they spied Pam's dad coming down the path from his farmhouse a quarter mile to the south.

"Hey, ladies!" he called.

"Hi, Dad!"

"Hi, Mr. Morgan," Greta said as they walked to meet him.

"Richard or Dick, please," he said, hugging them both. "There are no Mr. Morgans around here. I understand you're assisting our flower expert?"

"Happy to," Greta said, smiling at the tall, slender man with his thick salt-and-pepper hair, bushy eyebrows, and dark brown eyes. Handsome and always full of energy, he looked a decade younger than his fifty-six years.

"I see we're in the uniform of the day," Richard said, referring to their similar attire: jeans, green Field and Fire T-shirts, and sneakers.

"And we're ready to go," Pam said. "What's your assignment?"

"Gopher. Your husband just called to ask if I'd run some errands for them, so I'm here to get my assignment."

"Well, Lindels just arrived with all the indoor plants, so Greta and I have to get to it."

"Won't keep you. See you Friday night, if not before," he said, winking at Greta before heading around the building to the side door.

Pam had copies of the restaurant's interior, which she handed to the men as they began unloading. Once the plants were inside, the two women supervised placements, standing back to be sure, adjusting as needed. Sandy came in briefly while they worked, kissing his wife and saying hi to Greta, before heading over to the winery.

As they worked, Greta gazed around in awe at the beautiful spaces Sandy Rodriguez had created. When she asked Pam about who had designed the restaurant, she said proudly, "It's all my husband. His vision." The main dining room was divided into two large rooms, and there were three smaller function rooms to the south. Each space had walls of windows to the east affording unobstructed views of the river and fields. The decor was light and airy, with large dramatic botanical prints on the walls, painted light, muted pastel shades that blended with their exterior surroundings. The bar jutted out in a separate octagon to the north, its own entity.

There was also an extensive wine cellar behind glass, gleaming counters in light blonde mahogany, beautiful mosaic tiled tables, and comfortable chairs and barstools. The entire restaurant was lovely and understated, taking its inspiration from its exquisite surroundings.

The women worked for several hours, Greta constantly on edge that Murph might walk in, but he didn't. In fact no one even mentioned his name. She wasn't sure if she was relieved or disappointed, but as they packed up and grabbed their bags, the kitchen doors swung open, and there he was, a load of menus in his arms. He spied her friend first. "Hey, Pam. Looks terrific."

Pam smiled. "Thanks. Couldn't have done it without my buddy."

Murph suddenly noticed Greta, and his jaw dropped. "Oh... Hi, it's you. Didn't know you were helping."

Greta felt sick to her stomach, but managed to reply, "Yup, my pleasure." Her knees were trembling, and not the good kind of trembling, although he did look as handsome as ever in jeans and a plaid work shirt. He set down his load and crossed the room.

Pam said, "Hey, Murph, gotta run. I'll see you later." Before Greta could follow, her friend quickly skipped out.

Traitor, she thought, turning toward the front door, but not soon enough.

"How have you been?" he said, his nearness unnerving her.

"Fine, and you?" She straightened up, steeling herself to keep from blubbering.

"Busy."

"Well, congratulations on your new job. The restaurant looks incredible."

He regarded her with soft eyes. "Thanks."

After an awkward few seconds, Greta said, "Well, I came with Pam, so I'd better go. See ya." Her eyes filled with tears as she turned away.

"Greta, wait."

"See you!" she cried, hurrying out the front door without looking back.

~

MURPH WATCHED HER GO, THEN SAT HARD IN THE NEAREST CHAIR. *What the hell have I done? I had the beginning of an amazing relationship with the most beautiful, generous woman I've ever met, and I blew it.*

Sandy came out of the kitchen and grabbed a bottle of water from the cooler on the counter that they'd set out for workers. "Hey, buddy. What's up? You look like you just got the shit kicked out of you."

"I gave myself the kick."

"Say what?" His boss looked at him, a puzzled look on his face.

"Pam and Greta just left."

"Oh? How was that?"

"A nightmare."

"Did you talk to her?"

"What could I say? Besides, she ran out of here so fast, I barely got a word in."

His friend laughed, patting him on the shoulder. "Cheer up, the flower ladies'll be back Friday. You'll have plenty of time to catch up."

"Yeah, right."

"And Greta'll be at the opening."

"Is she coming with you guys?"

Sandy shook his head. "Since I'll be here all day, Pam's coming with her family. Her brother Ben's bringing Greta, I think."

"Good. At least she won't have to deal with a shit like me."

His friend watched him for a minute, then said, "Look, you can wallow all you want Saturday morning, but I need you all in for the next two days. I'm heading next door to talk to Wolfie. Wanna come?"

Murph stood. "Why not? The menus can wait. Are we bringing wine back? Do we need the hand truck?"

"We're good. Just trying to confirm procedures for restocking. You should hear it too."

Wolfie Morgan, Pam's youngest brother, managed Morgan's Fire Winery. He and his staff had been working overtime to get ready for the opening. They didn't yet have anywhere near the inventory the restaurant would need, but Wolfie had done all the liquor ordering.

In keeping with the farm-to-table commitment, most of the wines were from New England. They had some California wines and a few select imported labels. They had also ordered cases of Saguaro Valley wines, a vineyard owned by good friends of Pam and Wolfie's aunt and uncle. The bar walls were lined with beautifully framed photographs of most of their partner vineyards.

They found Wolfie in the tasting barn, talking with a group of visitors. Cara Feldspar, his assistant and an apprentice vintner, circulated, pouring wines. Wolfie spied them, signaled one minute with his finger, and returned his attention to his visitors. Five minutes later, he said, "Enjoy, folks. If you have any questions, just ask Cara. I should be available shortly."

"Hey," he said, approaching the two men.

"Morning," Sandy said. "Just checking on restocking. I'm sure we'll have plenty of everything, but someone will be here, right?"

"Well, I'll be over there. Just find me, and I can come back and grab whatever you need."

They spoke for a few minutes, then Wolfie walked them out. "Hey, I just saw my sister and Greta. Do you think they need help transporting flowers Friday morning?"

"I'll check with Pam," Sandy said. "She and Greta will both have trucks, so they should be fine."

"I was talking manpower."

Sandy laughed. "They're stronger than they look. Besides, they've already dropped off all the vases and whatever. They'll be bringing the flowers in buckets. I'm sure they'll be fine. Your brothers are gonna be around too, right?"

"Yeah, and Gerry will probably come with Teddy. My dad told me that Ben's bringing Greta. I didn't know they were an item."

"They aren't," Murph said, a bit more abruptly than he intended.

Both men looked at him.

Murph turned bright red. "I mean, I don't think they're an item."

Sandy stood back, watching his friend, then said, "Greta didn't want to come alone, so Ben offered. I don't think they've met more than once or twice."

Wolfie grinned. "That's Ben, all right. Always the chivalrous one."

"Well, thanks, Wolfie. We'll let you get back to it," Sandy said.

The two men headed for the door, and Wolfie went back to the tasting room.

Once outside, Sandy turned to him. "What the hell was that?"

Murph shrugged. "Don't start."

"Look, man, you've gotta fix this. I can't have you bouncing around like a pinball machine every time you set eyes on you-know-who. Anyone with half a brain can see that you're crazy about her, so it's time to shit or get off the pot. Talk to her! The silent treatment isn't working for either of you."

Murph waved his hand. "Fine, fine, I'll deal with it. Just give me time."

"I'm only thinking of you. She seems like a terrific person. You could do a lot worse."

"She is a great person. That's not it, and you know it."

CHAPTER 15

Most of the flowers for Field and Fire were coming from Laura's Community Garden, but Thursday afternoon, Pam and Greta had made a quick run to Lindels in Southport. They stored these flowers in one of the industrial refrigerators in what Pam's dad called the Morgan's Fire Party Barn. Early Friday, they picked all the blooms they needed from the community garden plots and headed to the farm.

They parked the two trucks and rounded the house, hoping to make a quick pickup, but Richard spotted them out the kitchen window and called, "Hey, gals, Callie's put out a huge breakfast buffet for our full house. Come on in and join us."

"Morning, Dad!" Pam called. "We've both eaten, but after we finish at the restaurant, we'll stop over and say hi."

Richard turned back to the house. "Hold on, I'm getting a shout. Your brothers, Gerry, and Gail say they'll be out in five. They'd like to lend a hand. If you wait, they can hop on the back of the trucks."

"Great," Pam called, turning to Greta. "Welcome to the joys of a large family."

"You are so lucky."

"I know. It's just a bit overwhelming sometimes. At least they can help with the unloading. Gerry and Gail can help with the arranging as they'll follow the models, but the other two will need to be redirected."

Greta laughed, following her into the barn. *How many thousands of times over the years have I wished for siblings?*

Half the plants were loaded when they were joined by the crew from the farmhouse. "Here we are," Pam's oldest brother Rich said, arms open wide. "Weezie says she can come if you need her."

Pam laughed, gazing at her sister Gail, her three brothers, and Teddy's partner, Gerry. "I think we're gonna be just fine. What do you think, Greta?"

Greta smiled, suddenly feeling like an outsider. "I agree. So nice to see you all."

Pam looked from her friend to her family. "I can't remember, have you all met Greta?"

"Just briefly," Greta said, "at the opening of the community garden. You probably don't remember me. That was a pretty crazy day and—"

"Of course we remember you." Teddy, the slight, sandy haired brother with blue eyes, came forward to hug her. "You remember my husband, Gerry?" he added, gesturing to the tall, wiry man beside him with brown hair and a trimmed brown beard.

"Yes, great to see you," Greta said, returning Gerry's embrace.

"My date!" Ben Morgan said, brushing straight dark hair from his brow as he stepped up to hug her. Tall and slender with the build of a runner, which he was, his green eyes were warm and soft.

"Yes, thank you for letting me tag along with your group."

"Nonsense," Gail said. "We're all looking forward to it." Pam's sister was short and petite, with curly auburn hair, hazel eyes, and freckles. All of them, including Gail, wore green Field and Fire T-shirts and jeans.

"Let's get to it," Pam said. "There are still eight buckets in the fridge."

With so many hands, the loading went quickly, then the others jumped onto the tailgates of the two trucks. When they arrived at Field and Fire, Pam gave a short speech about where the buckets should go and who would be doing what. As the others unloaded and took the buckets of flowers to the workroom behind the kitchen, Pam, Gail, Greta, and Gerry got together to discuss the arrangements. They decided that Pam would make a prototype for the tables and then they could begin the work. Much to his delight, Gerry was given carte blanche for design of the six large arrangements. One would go in each dining room, one in the bar and several near the entrance. Pam directed him to the buckets of flowers and vases they had designated for these more dramatic bouquets.

Under Pam's direction, the rest of the group began on the table arrangements. Teddy was assigned to fill the vases with water since his sisters declared him color blind and hopeless. The rest gathered around buckets of blooms at the worktables. Ben and Greta worked side by side, with him asking for her approval as he completed an arrangement. The gesture was unnecessary because he created each bouquet with the precision of the surgeon he was. Every vase was perfect, whereas Greta's were a bit more "free form."

"So Pam tells me you're completing your residency in Philadelphia?" she said, gazing over as he carefully snipped the stem on a brilliant orange zinnia.

Eyeing the flower, he grinned. "Four months to go."

"Then what?"

"Then I look for a job. I'm hoping for Boston Children's, but at this point, I'm open to anywhere."

"You're a surgeon, right?"

"Yup, pediatric. General surgery at the moment, but I'm also seeking fellowships. I'd eventually like to specialize in pediatric cardiac surgery."

"I think that flower you're holding should be the heart of that bouquet," she said, smiling.

"Oh, really? I've got a better idea." He leaned and tucked the zinnia behind her ear. "Perfect."

"I don't think your sister would agree," she said, flicking water at him as the kitchen door swung open and Murph walked in.

~

MURPH'S MOUTH DROPPED OPEN AS HE SPIED GRETA AND BEN laughing and flicking water at each other. Pam noticed the pair at the same moment, but rather than intervene, she continued with her work.

What the hell? Murph thought, turning his attention to Pam and Gail, who sat together just inside the door. "Hey, looks like you have quite a team here."

Pam waved to him. "Hi, Murph. I'm not sure, do you know my brothers Ben and Teddy, and Gerry, of course? Guys, this is Murph O'Neill, Sandy's right-hand man."

"Hey, guys. I think we've met at the club or around town, but it's been a while. Great to see everyone."

"Congratulations on the new job," Gail said. "We always knew Sandy'd get you over here."

"Thanks," he said, smiling at her. He didn't know Gail well, but sometimes crewed on her husband Tim Miller's lobster boat when he needed extra hands. "Where's your hubby today?"

"On the river, where else? The poachers never take a day off, so he doesn't feel he can either." Tim Miller divided his time between his workshop in town where he crafted one-of-a-kind furniture, and the river, where he lobstered and chased poachers who illegally caught and killed the native horseshoe crabs for bait.

Without looking in Greta's direction, he said, "Well, good luck. The flowers look incredible. The boss'll be thrilled."

"We hope so!" Pam said, waving as he hurried out the front door.

"That was odd," Gail whispered, exchanging looks with her sister.

Pam gazed across the room to find Greta staring after him, the color drained from her face. Ben was talking to her, but she didn't appear to be listening or even aware of his presence. "I believe it concerns my friend across the room."

"Greta?"

"She and Murph had a fling, a pretty hot one, but apparently, it's over. Very strange. Sandy says it's Murph's doing, but won't say why."

"Too bad," Gail whispered. "They'd make a great couple."

"Tell me about it," Pam said.

Teddy regarded them sharply. "Hey, what are you two whispering about?"

"How bad you are as a florist?" Gail said.

"Ha-ha," her brother said, throwing a clump of greenery across the table.

"Earth to Greta," Ben said.

Shaking herself, she looked at him. "Oh, sorry. Lost in space."

"Seemed like Mr. O'Neill triggered the sudden journey to another galaxy?"

"Got me. Pretty obvious, huh? We had a thing. It seemed like a great thing, actually, and then he cut me off, and I have no idea why."

"He's a fool."

She shrugged. "Maybe. Anyway, it's still a bit of an awkward situation. That's kind of why I didn't want to come alone tonight. Thanks for being my escort."

"Escort, huh? Sounds promising."

She flicked more water at him. "You know what I mean."

"Well, let's give Mr. Murphy O'Neill something to think about, shall we?"

Greta gave him a look. "I'd rather just get through the night in one piece."

Ben grinned, twirling a white snapdragon in front of her. "Done."

Murph's stomach lurched as he closed the door behind him, and he bent over, afraid he might vomit. *How the hell am I going to get through tonight with her on Ben Morgan's arm? Smart, successful, handsome, and rich Ben Morgan? He's a doctor, for Pete's sake!*

"Uh-oh, what's wrong now?" Sandy called as he hopped out of his truck. "Don't tell me it's your love life again."

Murph stood up straight and waved him off. "Forget it. I'm headed into town. Meryl needs a few things, and I gotta stop at home."

Sandy approached, barring his way. "You're gonna talk to her tomorrow, right? Clear the air? You'll both feel better."

Murph stepped around him. "I'll be back."

"With a smile on your face!" his boss called. "We've got a lot riding on tonight."

Smile, right. I may have to get some glue to keep a smile on my pathetic face.

CHAPTER 16

Field and Fire officially opened its doors at four o'clock on Friday afternoon. Sandy greeted guests as they arrived, and Pam stood nearby, saying hello. His family were some of the first to appear. Rosa and Cesar Rodriguez had closed their restaurant, the Grille, for the evening and were accompanied by three of their offspring, Raffi, an attorney, Vincent, who worked at the Grille, and Milania, "Milly," who lived at home and waitressed at the Café and the Grille.

Rosa hugged her son. "Proud of you, Santiago. Now don't take all our business away."

"Thanks, Mama."

"Where have you put us? Near all the Yarners, I hope?" An original member of the Darn Yarners, Rosa rarely got a night off to be with her friends.

"You guys are with the Yarners, and Raffi, Vin, and Milly are at a kids' table."

His father embraced him. "Hey, son, how about a look at the kitchen in action?"

Sandy cringed. "Mmm, Meryl's pretty fussy about who goes in there while she's cooking."

Cesar patted him on the shoulder. "Just kidding."

"Well, stop," his wife said. "'Cause I'm starving. I want wine and some of those incredible appetizers I just saw go by. Come on."

"Congrats, bro. This is awesome," Raffi said as he followed the others. Dark and gorgeous like his big brother, with coal-black bedroom eyes, he was one of many village heartthrobs.

The staff bustled about with Murph circulating between rooms, checking in with bartenders, waiters, and waitresses and other floating staff. His parents were also among the first to arrive, Fiona and Murphy Senior, along with Murph's siblings, Seamus and Darby.

"Well, don't you look smart," his mother said, standing back to admire the beige linen suit he'd purchased especially for tonight. His crisp white shirt was already irritating his neck, but he smiled.

"Thanks, Mum." He straightened his tie, then yanked the knot down so he could breathe.

As his father and siblings drifted off to the bar, Fiona O'Neill gazed at her son, eyes full of concern. "Everything okay, love?"

"Fine. Just a lot to keep track of."

"Is your girl coming tonight? We're looking forward to meeting her."

His eyes scanned the room before meeting hers. "She's not my girl. I screwed that one up like I always do."

"Oh, son, I'm sorry."

He gave her a rueful smile. "My lot in life, Mum. We've always known that."

She placed her hand on his forearm. "No, we haven't. You're the only one who thinks that way. Certainly your father and I don't, and your brother and sister don't remember her and that terrible time."

"Well, I do," he said, shrugging out of her grasp.

"Aislan wouldn't want this for you."

"We'll never know, will we?"

Hands on hips, she gave him a sharp look. "Murphy O'Neill, don't you dare use that sweet girl to justify your foolish, misguided behavior."

Her words struck hard, but as more people streamed in, he simply replied, "Look, I can't have this conversation now. Want me to locate your table?"

"No, I'll find your father and then check the place cards. You go."

As he turned to the crowded room, she touched his shoulder. "Maybe you should talk to Father Joseph."

"You know I've left the church."

"That doesn't mean you can't seek counsel from the priest who's known you practically since birth."

She turned away and headed for the bar, leaving him adrift as he gazed toward the door and spied the Morgan contingent, Greta on Ben's arm in the center of them. *Here goes*, he thought, heading in the opposite direction as his boss greeted his in-laws.

GRETA SPIED HIM FROM THE DOORWAY, AND HER HEART SKIPPED A BEAT. There could be two hundred people in the room and she was certain she'd find him. Her senses always went on high alert when he was around. "Hey, you okay?" Ben asked, noticing her gaze. "He's heading in the opposite direction, so you can relax."

Blushing, she turned to him. "Some date, huh?"

He gave her a soft smile. "I'm not complaining. Come on, let's find out where they've put this unwieldy group of ne'er-do-wells.

After finding their table, the men went off to get drinks for everyone, even though servers were circulating constantly. Greta sat beside Pam, resting her head for a second against her friend's shoulder. "I should have stayed home."

"No way. Besides, he gone. Probably hiding in the kitchen."

"Can't stay in there all night. Every time I see him, I want to throw up."

"Well, you'll be on an airplane to sunny California tomorrow morning, and you can put a certain hunky manager out of your mind."

"Slight change of plans," Greta said, meeting Pam's eyes.

"Oh?"

"Sarah's asked me to stay for two months. She had a fall and needs the help."

"Two months! That's the whole summer."

"Tell me about it. Summer's my favorite time here."

"What about Daisy?"

"The Crockers were going to take her for the two weeks, so I'm sure they'll extend. I think they miss her. Who am I kidding? I'll miss her. I've gotten so attached to her."

"What about your house? Your beautiful gardens?"

"I know, I know, but how can I say no to Aunt Sarah? She's such a sweetheart. I'm actually looking for someone who might like to house sit for the summer."

"You know, I might have some who'd be interested," Pam said, smiling as Gerry handed her a glass of white wine.

"Really, who?"

"Have you met Jack Faulkner? His company's developing Barnum's Ledge."

"You mean the guy who's engaged to Lucy's partner?" Greta referred to Lolly Rogers, who owned and ran a very successful book company, Merlin's Closet, with Pam's stepmother, Lucy Morgan. Merlin's Closet was mostly a mail-order business selling children's books and adult regional mysteries, but they also ran local book fairs at schools and libraries.

Pam nodded. "Yup."

"You mean one of the most gorgeous middle-aged guys around?"

Pam laughed. "That's the one. Anyway, his daughter Lyddie has a thing going with Wolfie and Lucy just told me she's been looking for summer jobs in the village. She just put in an application for a job here. I wouldn't be surprised if she comes tonight."

"Sounds promising. I'll be on the lookout or get her contact info from Lucy or Lolly. The upshot of all these changed plans is that I'm not leaving till the end of this week, so I have time to make all these arrangements. Sarah's son, Ralph Junior, is with her now, but he's needed at home. His wife's going crazy."

"Well, I'm glad you're sticking around a few days. We'll have time for a lunch or ride, and you and Murph can find a moment to clear the air."

"Yes to lunch and a ride, but as for clearing the air with you-know-who, that's wishful thinking."

CHAPTER 17

The evening was a huge success, with people oohing and aahing about Meryl's food, the décor, the flowers and amazing views from every table. Frankie Brown sat with Lucy's mom, Helen, at the Darn Yarners' table, gazing around the main dining room. "Look at how your son-in-law Richard has changed the landscape around here," Frankie said.

Helen nodded, watching her daughter laughing with Wolfie, his arm draped around a lovely young woman.

"That's for sure," Belle Pollart said, raising her glass. "Our sleepy little town is still the way we love it, but with some major additions. How did we do without the community garden or party central over here at Morgan's Fire?"

"Richard still appreciates the qualities that make small towns special," Helen said.

"Looks like the youngest Morgan has a serious girlfriend," Belle said. "Who is she?"

"Jack Faulkner's daughter Lydia. She's here for the summer, I understand," Helen said. "Have you met Jack?"

"He's engaged to my daughter," Mavis LaSalle said, eavesdropping from across the table.

"Lolly's engaged?" Belle said. "I have been out of it lately with the docks and fish market so busy."

Mavis nodded. "Yes, and she's happier than I've ever seen her. Jack's a calming influence on my baby." Mavis's forty-year-old daughter, Lolly, still lived in one of the cottages on her mother's estate. Her fiancé, Jack, still rented next door as they waited for their new home on Barnum's Ledge to be completed. Jack was managing the renovation and new construction out at the Inn and cottages at the southwest edge of the village.

As the friends watched, Greta and Pam approached Lucy and her companions. "How's poor Greta doing?" Mavis asked to no one in particular. "I've always felt guilty that we didn't ask her mom to join the Darn Yarners."

"We did," Belle said. "Don't you remember? She politely declined. Said she was too busy with her family and property."

"She was shy, I think," Helen said. "And maybe we asked at a time when she didn't need us. Goodness knows if I hadn't found this gang, I probably wouldn't have survived," she added, gazing around the table at her dear friends.

"You can say that again!" Mavis said. "Greta looks well, doesn't she? She was kind of a scrawny little girl, but she's grown into a lovely young woman. Ugly duckling to swan?"

Helen waved her hand. "In my recollection, Greta was never ugly."

Mavis sniffed, nodding. "Just different, I guess."

"THAT WOULD BE AMAZING," LYDIA SAID, AFTER GRETA ASKED HER ABOUT housesitting. After Pam introduced them, she stepped away to allow the two women time to chat. "I've been looking for jobs. I'd planned to live with my dad, but he's engaged and would probably appreciate the space."

"I'd love for you to come out and see the place," Greta said, giving her the address and simple directions. "Are you available tomorrow?"

"Absolutely. What time?"

As they talked, Murph stood nearby talking to Wolfie. He overheard Greta say, "There is one thing. I have a pet goat. Would that be a problem?"

"Are you kidding? I love animals!"

"I might be able to make other arrangements if she'd tie you down."

"I can't imagine how, but I can meet her tomorrow, and you can tell me about her care. There's my dad waving me to our table. See you in the morning? So excited!"

As Lyddie hurried off, Murph came to her side. "You're going away?"

"Yes," Greta replied.

"Why didn't you let me know? I could have watched Daisy."

"Says the person who's barely spoken to me in weeks. Why would I ask you?"

"Look, Greta, maybe sometime we could talk?"

His hand brushed against her arm, and she shivered. "Maybe, but right now, I've got to get to my table. Excuse me." As she practically ran across the room, she let out the breath she'd been holding. *Be strong!* she thought, catching Ben's eye as he watched her draw near.

CHAPTER 18

Greta's doorbell rang just before eleven. With Daisy at her side bleating happily, she opened the door to find Lydia on the stoop with a handsome, broad-shouldered, older man, with the same sandy hair as her own with extraordinary blue eyes. "This is my dad, Jack Faulkner," said the slender young woman, her hazel eyes twinkling. Both were in shorts and T-shirts, the daughter in flip-flops, her dad in worn boat shoes.

Greta had seen Jack around the village but never formally met him. "Hi, great to see you both. Come on in. This is Daisy," she added, stooping to grab the kid's collar should she decide to bolt out the door.

"Hey, you!" Lydia said, scooping up the tiny goat and cradling her in her arms. "You're the most adorable thing I've ever seen!"

"Farm girl at heart," her father said, flashing a gorgeous smile.

Lolly Rogers is one lucky woman! Greta mused as she led them through the house. "This is it. I've hired Kevin Averill to take care of the grass and trimming, and I have a housekeeper who comes every two weeks. My one indulgence. She's been with my family for years, Bessie."

"What a great spot," he said, peering out one of the east windows. "Amazing views."

"It was my parents' home. They renovated it from top to bottom. They put in all the gardens and landscaping. It was truly a labor of love for them."

They stepped out on the terrace and watched Lyddie roll around the grass with Daisy. Jack whistled. "Wow, what a yard. Is it just you here?"

"I'm an only child, so yes."

He smiled at her. "So whatever possessed you to get a goat?"

"She was a gift from some grateful parents. I fully intended to give her back or find a farm that could take her, but I've gotten kind of attached to her. I'm really going to miss her this summer."

"Yeah, Lyddie said you're going to be away for almost two months?"

"My aunt isn't well. She asked me to come. She's one of my only family left. My mom and dad both passed away last year."

"I'm so sorry to hear that," he said.

"Thanks. It's been tough, but I'm doing better now."

"So how's your little critter been with the gardens? Has she been nibbling?"

"Surprisingly not."

"She's adorable," Lyddie said, approaching them. "Is this as big as she's going to get?"

"Just about. She's a small breed, a Tennessee fainting goat, which means that sometimes she has these spells where she'll just stop and stand still for a minute or two. She often falls over, like she's fainted."

"Oh, poor baby," Lyddie said, sitting beside Daisy on the grass.

"It's normal for the breed. It doesn't hurt her, so don't be alarmed if and when she does it. She stays outside most of the day. If I leave, I makes sure she has food and water in the shed. and I always give her a few treats—carrots, celery, grapes, whatever I have. I'll leave a list and some vegetables to get you started."

"We'll be just fine, won't we, Daisy?" the young woman said, burying her face in the goat's thick black hair.

"Already in love," her father said.

"Well, if she becomes too much or you go away, I'll leave the Crockers' phone number. They said they'll take her anytime."

"Too bad my yard isn't fenced, or she could absolutely stay with me," Jack said.

Greta smiled at him. "I'm sure the Crockers will be fine as backup. Truth be told, I think they miss her. She's quite a character."

"I can see that. So you've lived in the village your whole life?"

"No, my parents moved here about ten years ago. I grew up in Newton."

"One of my old stomping grounds, among many others. What do you do for work?"

"I'm a social worker at the high school."

"Tough job."

"Sometimes. It was tougher when I lived in Boston doing my grad school practicum. Our case load was draconian."

"I've heard that about city agencies. So you escaped to Horseshoe Crab Cove?"

"Actually, I escaped to a fancy clinic north of Boston, Farrell Park. They specialize in—"

"Eating disorders," he interrupted.

Greta stared at him in surprise. "You know Farrell Park?"

"Small world, I guess. I knew someone...know someone who's there. The daughter of my ex-girlfriend."

Lyddie had wandered off toward the shed with Daisy.

"How's she doing?"

"Better, I hope. For a lot of reasons, her social worker and I decided it was best if I cease contact with her. Truth is, I barely know Poppy, but the poor kid hasn't a lot of options."

"I'm sorry to hear that."

"So, why'd you leave Farrell?"

"Many reasons. Farrell Park is really good at what they do, but I wanted school-based work. I probably would have stayed on for a few more years, but my parents needed me here."

"It sure is a beautiful spot."

They talked awhile longer, then father and daughter said their goodbyes. Greta gave Lyddie keys to the house and promised to email instructions and touch base on Thursday. As she waved them out of the driveway, Greta felt the familiar pang of loneliness. Murph had helped ease that for a very short time, and now it was back full force. As she stepped into the house, her cell phone rang.

"Hey, it's me," he said.

Greta had already read "Murph," so she knew it was him. "Hi."

"I was wondering if you're free tomorrow? The restaurant's closed on Monday. Maybe we could grab coffee or something?"

"When were you thinking?"

"Anytime that works for you."

"Where?"

"I was thinking Sebring Park? I could grab us something and meet you there."

"Why don't we say two."

"Great. I'll stop at the Café on my way through town. What can I get you?"

A new life, she thought, but said, "A medium iced green tea would be great, thanks."

"Anything in it?"

"Plain's fine."

"Well, I'll see you then."

As she clicked off her phone, Greta wondered if meeting with him was a mistake. Then she shrugged, threw the phone on the counter, and opened the fridge to make lunch. *We have to bump into each other is this tiny town. Maybe clearing the air is a good thing.*

CHAPTER 19

Greta was seated on a bench in the shade at Sebring Park when Murph arrived. "Hey," he said, handing her the iced tea.

"Thanks." She reached into her pocket for the monkfruit sweetener she used.

He sat beside her, and they gazed out at the ocean in silence for several minutes in the small green space created years earlier through the fundraising and labor of the Darn Yarners and friends. It had a covered, terraced pavilion area near the cliffs, with eight benches and two acres of landscaped walkways and plantings behind it.

"Good choice of venue," she said, gazing around them. They were alone in the pavilion and only a handful of people roamed the park, all strangers.

"Yeah, better for a quiet talk than the Crab Café."

She nodded. "Well, it's your party."

"Yeah, it is." Murph swallowed hard. "Greta, I'm really sorry about all this."

She turned to him, a lump in her throat. "I have no idea what all this is, so I don't know what to say or think. I don't ordinarily hop into bed with men I hardly know, not to mention screwing a virtual stranger in a public place. It's not me at all."

"I know."

"I trusted you."

"I know."

"So, what do you want to talk about?"

"It's a long story, but I'll try to explain. I had something happen when I was young. It was pretty traumatizing. I've never really gotten over it, I guess. It keeps me from getting close to people, especially women, and you and I got close real fast. It spooked me. Sent me right back to where I can't go."

Greta watched him rubbing his hands, the knuckles turning white. "If it's really painful, don't feel like you have to tell me. I mean...if it's too much."

"No, I want to. It's...it was... Well, I think I've told you that I have a brother and sister, Seamus and Darby, right?"

She nodded.

"Well, I also had another sister. Aislan, my twin. We were kind of inseparable. We had our own language like twins often do. I mean, we talked English to other people, but with each other, it was different. My parents tried to help us be more independent, encouraged other friendships, interactions with neighbors' kids and our cousins, but it was no good. We clung to each other as if we were physically joined.

"Our farm was right on the river. One afternoon when we were six, Aislan and I were playing by the river, making boats. Our parents were nearby in the yard. I convinced her to climb the rise that led to the cliffs. She didn't like it up there. She was afraid of heights, but she'd do anything for me.

"We climbed to the top and played around a while. She kept asking to go back, but I refused. I teased her and called her a baby, cajoling until she agreed her to stay a little longer. Finally, she turned and started running down the path. There are a couple of places where it's really narrow with a steep drop-off. I'd almost caught up with her when she slipped and went over the edge. I grabbed for her, but she was gone. A straight drop into the river below. She never made a sound. Just the splash when she hit the water.

"I called to my dad and he came running, but the current took her, and she was just gone. They didn't find her for three days."

"Oh, Murph, I'm so sorry. How tragic and heartbreaking for you." She grasped his forearm as she gazed up, spying tears streaming down his face.

"As I said, it was a long time ago, but it's left me one screwed-up guy."

"Of course it would have. Have you had or did you have counseling at any point?"

"My parents did. They took me to some play therapy, but I don't think it helped much."

"Maybe it's time to try again?"

"Maybe. My mom's pushing me to see our priest. What a joke."

"Maybe not."

He shrugged. "Anyway, that's my story. I thought you should know. At least now you know that my defection has absolutely nothing to do with you. You're perfect. I miss you so much it hurts, but those few days with you dredged everything up, and I've been a mess ever since."

"I'm sorry," she said.

"Yeah, you know what?" he said, standing and suddenly shrugging her arm away. "I've got to go. I'm really sorry. I wanted to tell you, but I can't talk about this or us."

Staring up at him, Greta's heart ached. *Impossible relationships. That's my lot in life, I guess.*

"I'm gonna go. Thanks for listening," he said. Before she could utter another word, he turned away and hurried to his truck.

Greta sat for a long time, staring out at the sea. She wanted to cry, but she couldn't. The day was warm, yet she felt chilled to the bone. Finally, as she stood and walked to her truck, a tear trickled down her cheek, followed by a torrent. She slipped into the front seat, resting her head on the steering wheel, and sobbed. Thirty minutes later, she sat up, dried her eyes, turned the key, and drove away, back home to Daisy, who waited, bleating happily in the backyard. *Thank goodness for Daisy*, she thought, sighing.

CHAPTER 20

"How are you holding up?" Pam asked as the two friends carried their takeout from the Café to the community garden.

"Okay. All packed. I chatted with Lydia, and she's ready to move right in. I gave her your name and number in case of emergency."

"Good. Happy to be on call. There's a shady spot," Pam said as they passed under the archway at the garden's entrance.

Once they settled on one of the garden benches, Pam turned to her. "I guess Murph's been almost comatose this week. Sandy's worried about him."

"I'm sorry to hear that. What a tragic thing. Poor guy."

"I think he's more traumatized at losing you."

"Maybe, but I don't know what else to do. I've called him and left a couple of messages just telling him I'm thinking about him and that I care. That's pretty much all I can think of to do at this point."

"You're right. Give him time. Sandy's pushing therapy, but Murph's pretty stubborn. My colleague Elise is a great therapist, but he's got to take the first step."

"I'm surprised his family hasn't pushed harder."

"From what Sandy's said, his mom has tried over the years, but she's had a lot on her plate. After Aislan died, Murphy Senior's drinking got really bad. It's only in recent years that he's turned things around. When he and Sandy were in college, Murph was still a mess. He spent most vacations at the Rodriguezes'."

"What about his siblings?"

"They're younger and don't really remember Aislan. Darby, his sister, lives in Ohio, and Seamus got out of town as soon as he could. Went to college in Hawaii and has never come back."

"Oh, how sad. I mean, I don't know what it's like to have siblings, but it must be hard not to see each other."

"Murph's been to visit Seamus a couple of times."

"So how's the restaurant's first week been?'

"Phenomenal. People have come from all over, and it's gotten three great reviews. Some big Boston food critic's supposed to be coming next week. My normally calm husband's about to crawl out of his skin."

"Has this been a good move for Sandy? The restaurant business is brutal. Does he regret selling Sandy's?"

"Not for a second. I think his plan is to hire two managers, Murph and someone else, so they can spell each other and no one gets burned out. Then he thinks he can step back a little. I'll believe it when I see it."

"Then there's his chef. How's he going to keep Meryl from burning out?"

"I think the long-term plan is to hire a second chef, but Meryl's kind of a control freak, so I'm not sure how that'll work. At least she has a large staff to share the workload."

The friends chatted for an hour or so before Greta said, "I've got to get going. Last-minute stuff and all." She stood and discarded her sandwich wrapper in a nearby barrel. "I'll miss you and everyone."

"We'll write and text and email. If there's anything to tell, I'll be in touch."

"Thanks," Greta said, smiling as they hugged goodbye in the parking lot next to the garden.

"I still think there's hope," Pam said.

"Always the optimist," Greta said, hopping into the truck. "Take care of yourself, and fingers crossed that Field and Fire continues to be a huge success."

KEVIN AVERILL, SON OF GENERAL STORE OWNER HANK AVERILL, DROVE her to Logan Airport Friday morning. As they drove up the Coast Road toward the highway, Greta's heart ached. Two months was a long time to be away, and she had shed more than a few tears saying goodbye to Daisy. She had left her pet in the backyard with lots of hugs and treats to await Lyddie's arrival in an hour or so.

CHAPTER 21

Three weeks after Greta's departure, Murph pulled up to his parents' farm for Sunday dinner. Since he started at the restaurant, he hadn't gotten out to the farm much. As he parked, he noticed a strange car in the driveway. Sundays, it was usually only the three of them. His mother greeted him as he stepped onto the porch. "Hello, love. Guess who'll be joining us today?" She stepped aside, and Murph spied Joseph O'Leary, the parish priest. A young fifty, O'Leary rose from his seat in the living room and came to greet him.

"Hello, young Murphy. Haven't seen you in a while." He was tall, lanky, and handsome, his dark brown eyes warm, his handshake firm. Although he'd preached two services already and would preside over the five o'clock mass, the priest was in jeans, sport shirt, and well-worn running shoes.

"Hey, Father Joe, good to see you," Murph said, returning the handshake. Joseph O'Leary held a special place in the family's heart for the gentle, loving way he had handled Aislan's service as a first year parish priest and his daily visits to their home for months after her death. Despite his mother's obvious meddling, it was good to see him.

Over a dinner of roast lamb, new potatoes, and the most exotic salad Murph had eaten in months, they discussed all kinds of things, from the new restaurant to happenings in Bayport.

As Murph speared a chunk of spicy nasturtium leaves, he said, "Do you have a nasturtium crop big enough to supply Field and Fire? Meryl would go crazy for these."

His father nodded. "We've been lucky so far. Biggest yield yet, and the season's just getting started. Take a bag to your chef. See what she thinks, and we'll talk."

The O'Neills specialized in growing exotic herbs, roots, flowers, vegetables, and fruits, which they supplied to restaurants and specialty markets as far away as New York. His mom was also a popular mystery writer who had come to the marriage with a sizable inheritance. Between her family money, writing income, sale of the very popular O'Neill's Pub in Bayport, and the farm harvest, the family had lived well.

After a dessert of luscious Irish cream cheesecake, Murph declined coffee and excused himself to go outside and take a call from Sandy. His boss wondered if he'd be free to come for a brief meeting at four thirty. He agreed and clicked off, gazing out over the farm's back fields which were green and lush as far as the eye could see.

"God's country for certain."

Joe's voice startled him as he'd been unaware of the priest's approach. "Yup," he said. "Changes so much every time I come. I barely recognize it."

"How 'bout a tour?" the priest said.

"Not sure I'm the right person for that job, but I'll give it a try," Murph said as they started off toward the nearest field of herbs and flowers. The scent of lavender surrounded them as they brushed against pale purple mounds that lined this part of the garden. "My mom grows like thirty different kinds of lavender."

"I buy her lavender essential oil whenever it's available," Joe said. "Best sleep aid on the planet."

"Can't believe that priests have trouble sleeping. Clear consciences and all."

The other man laughed. "Ah, the myths that surround us."

"Which ones are those?" Murph asked, smiling. "The sleeping or clear conscience?"

"Both. From the looks of you, sleep has been a bit elusive lately," Joe said. "Long hours at the new restaurant?"

Murph shrugged. "I've been working long hours my whole adult life."

"Something else, then?"

Murph paused next to an arbor covered with pale pink roses, the entrance to the east flower beds. "I'm sure my mum's filled you in on my pathetic state."

"A little. Is that the reason for the sleeplessness, then?"

"Yup."

"Want to talk about it?"

"Not sure I know how. You saw the nightmare as it unfolded all those years ago. It never goes away." Murph indicated a stack of hay, and the two men sat side by side. "It's okay for Seamus and Darby. They don't remember her. But for me... Every time I touch a woman. Every time I get close to a woman, it all comes back. I can't... I couldn't... If I get close to someone and something happens and I can't get to her... I'm not sure I could come back from that again."

The priest met his gaze, his eyes sad. "You know when Aislan died, I seriously considered leaving the priesthood."

"You're kidding? That was like your first year, wasn't it?"

"Yup. I was just eighteen months out of seminary."

"So what made you stay?"

"Families like yours and the hope that I could bring solace and comfort. Help people to go on with their lives."

"And we have. I mean, my parents are like hollow-shell people sometimes, but they keep busy and so do I. The other two got sick of being around us and got out of Dodge."

"But you stayed?"

"My best friend is here... A lot of friends actually. And my work."

"And Aislan?"

"Yup, her too. I try to visit her once a month, but lately, I've been slipping."

"I visit her too," Joe said quietly.

Murph looked at him with surprise.

"Every time I walk the cemetery, I visit her."

"That's kind of you."

"Maybe... I suspect I do it for me as much as Aislan."

"Do you ever regret not having kids? Not getting married?"

"Sometimes. I've questioned my faith many times over the past few decades. I'm still not sure that the priesthood will be my life."

"Better not tell your congregation. They'll stage a revolt."

"I'm not going anywhere soon."

They sat in silence for several minutes. The breeze had stopped, and a hawk's cry pierced the quiet. Finally, Murph said, "Do you think there's any way to get beyond this?"

"Are you trying to get beyond or get closer to her? There's a difference, I think."

"Trouble is I'm not sure what that is. The difference, I mean. It's not like I see Aislan's face or her personality in Greta. I just fell hard for her quickly, and it scared me. Then I start to question if falling hard is about trying to bring Aislan back. To bring back what we had. How screwed up is that?"

"Maybe that's where you should begin."

"Excuse me?"

"You can never get Aislan back or the special bond you two had. That's gone forever. No woman is going to replicate that, nor should she. Mature love is a whole different animal. And, in truth, you have no idea where life and that bond would have taken you had she lived."

"Yeah, I know all that on a rational level, but emotionally? Maybe not. That's when things get fuzzy, blurred, and then I go haywire."

"I know your parents took you to a child therapist back then, but I wonder if a trauma specialist or grief counselor might help you now, as an adult?"

"Aren't I looking at one?"

The priest laughed. "After all these years, I have a fair amount of experience dealing with grief, although each situation is different, but trauma? Not so much. There's a really good person in Bayport. She's a conventional therapist, but she also has lots of training and experience in trauma therapy. Her name's Carroll Ranglund. I think the world of her."

"Sounds like you know her pretty well," Murph said, eyeing his companion.

"Let's just say that Carroll has pulled me from the abyss more than once." Joe reached into his pocket and pulled out a business card, then handed it to Murph. "I brought this along, just in case."

"Thanks." He pocketed the card, doubting he'd ever use it, but what the heck.

They talked awhile longer, then Joe checked his watch and said he needed to get back to prep for mass. He and Murph circled back along the vegetable beds, then headed for the house. Both men said their goodbyes to the O'Neills and each other and headed for the driveway. Fiona called her son back and handed him a small cooler with bags of nasturtium leaves and flowers and a few slices of her cake in a plastic container.

He accepted the cooler and hugged her again. "Thanks, Mum."

"Was Joe helpful?"

"Yup."

"So you're not angry at me for inviting him?"

"When have I ever been angry with you?"

"Oh, Lawd—get on with ya!" She slapped his shoulder, grinning.

As he drove toward Morgan's Fire, Murph felt a little lighter in spirit and wondered if he'd sleep any better tonight.

CHAPTER 22

Greta's days in California quickly fell into an easy rhythm based on her aunt's needs including help around the house and running errands. Sarah Jeffers lived in Carmel by the Sea in one of the beautiful cottages for which the village was known. Quaint, colorful homes lined the narrow streets and gave the village a fairy-tale like quality in the shadow of the larger, more metropolitan Monterey. Sarah's cottage had been recently renovated to accommodate her wheelchair, even though she rarely used it now. Mostly she hobbled around with a cane, but she still needed help with stairs and carrying heavy loads.

Several times a week, the women would head out in the early morning to markets and farm stands and to do any other errands Sarah might have. Greta always drove and found maneuvering Sarah's Suburban somewhat challenging. Several times, she had suggested to her aunt that they might go car shopping for a small vehicle, but Sarah waved her away, saying that she never knew when she would need the space to haul something. Greta spoke to her cousin Ralph, Sarah's son, almost every day with questions and concerns. He agreed about the car and promised to come for a visit soon so the two of them could stage what he called "a car intervention."

During the down times, she thought of home, Daisy, and, of course, Murph. How would she ever stop thinking about him? Lydia assured her that Daisy and the house and gardens were doing fine. Pam's texts and emails sometimes mentioned Murph, but had little of substance about him as she suspected her friend knew little. *Better this way*, she mused as Sarah called from the terrace.

"Let's take a beach walk, dearie. What do you say? We can try on that new beach wheelchair of mine if you don't mind pushing me."

Greta grinned at her aunt, seeing glimpses of her mother in the diminutive blonde with green eyes and a dazzling smile. "Love to!"

Murph waited a week, then called and made an appointment with Carroll Ranglund. She had an opening the following Monday, so he took it. Her office in Bayport was in a two-story Victorian on a quiet tree-lined street of older homes. He rang the bell, and the woman herself opened the door, ushering him into a hallway of muted colors and faded wallpaper. "I'm Carroll," she said. "My space is upstairs."

Middle-aged with salt-and-pepper hair, Ranglund was of medium build. She wore neat, faded jeans, sandals, and a flowing white muslin blouse. As he followed her, the scent of sandalwood surrounded him. Her consulting room was at the end of the hall. They passed a small kitchen and restroom, as well as what appeared to be a massage space. "Come in," she said, stepping aside to welcome him into a light-filled room with overstuffed upholstered chairs and a few side tables, including one holding a teapot, a basket of tea bags, and mugs in various shapes and sizes. There was also a small fridge in the corner.

"Would you like something to drink? I have tea or bottles of cold water?"

"Water would be great, thanks," he said.

She grabbed two waters from the fridge and invited him to sit. He sank down in one of the overstuffed chairs and tried to relax.

"So how did you find me and how can I help?"

"Father O'Leary recommended you."

"Joe's a dear friend."

Feeling awkward and increasingly nervous, Murph asked, "So how does this work?"

"That depends on you, Murphy. Is it okay for me to call you that or would you prefer Mr. O'Neill?"

"Most people call me Murph. One thing I know for certain is that I'm not a therapist, so I'll have to take my cues from you, if that's okay."

"Of course. You've come to me with something that's unsettling you, perhaps?"

"Did Joe tell you anything about me?"

"No. Why don't you tell me."

Murph gulped his water, then set the bottle on the table beside him. "Would it be okay if I just told you my story?"

"Of course," she said, smiling warmly.

He talked and talked until there seemed to be nothing more to say, ending with, "I miss Greta, and I've screwed things up just like I have with every woman I've ever dated. The others were easier. The difference now is that I love Greta, and I don't want to let her go."

"So you're wanting to take steps to make this one work?"

"Yes. Do you think it's possible?"

"You experienced a major life trauma losing your Aislan. That takes a special kind of healing. The good news is that that the human spirit and heart are very resilient. They can heal and grow stronger. I'd recommend both talk therapy of the kind you and I are doing now, but also energy work similar to reiki and some release work through qi gong. Have you heard of it?"

He shook his head.

"It's a specific kind of chanting aimed at releasing and healing the heart, mind and spirit. I hold a group class once a week. If you'd like to try, you'd be welcome to join us. I'd like to do an energy session or two before that, though, if you're willing?"

"Can I be honest?" Murph asked.

"Please."

"It all sounds like a bunch of mumbo jumbo, but at this point, I'd be willing to try anything."

The therapist nodded, reaching for a datebook on her table. After consulting together, they found four appointment times, and Murph thanked her, standing to go.

"You think there's hope for me and Greta?"

"Sometimes closeness helps the healing," she said. "And it sounds like you have time to work on your healing with her away. This might be the best place to start."

"Yes," he said, turning to go.

CHAPTER 23

After three sessions with Carroll Ranglund, some of which Murph would have labeled "mumbo jumbo" or "new agey," he made a decision that was partially prompted by a conversation with the therapist. During one of their regular sessions, she wondered aloud why he didn't at least contact Greta, even if it was just a phone call to say hello. That very night, he called Greta. After they'd chatted about the mundane, the call ended with him saying how good it was to hear her voice. Several days later, he called again, this time telling her a little about his work with Carroll. She wished him well. Several more calls later, he asked if he could come out to see her. "It will have to be a short visit because of Field and Fire."

Greta hesitated, but then said, "Why not?" With her aunt's help, she located the number of a B and B right down the street from Sarah's cottage and gave it to him. "We're just here hanging out, so plan your trip whenever is good for you and let me know."

Murph walked into the restaurant office the following morning at eight, still amazed that he'd proposed the California visit. He found Sandy and Meryl chatting about the day's menu. "Hey," he said. "Am I late?"

"No," his friend said. "I'm early, and I've got to run in a bit to take Maisie to camp. She's playing in the bar."

With a nod, Meryl stood and disappeared through the kitchen door.

Sandy eyed him. "What's up? You look like you have something on your mind."

Murph waved his arm dismissively. "We can talk later if you're in a hurry."

"I'm not. Maisie doesn't have to been there till nine."

"I was wondering... I mean, I know it's huge ask, and well, I wouldn't be doing it if ... Well, what I wondered is—could I take a few days off?"

"When?"

"Whatever days would be least disruptive."

"You know I'm all about my employees, especially you, but now? Can I ask what's going on?"

"Well, you know I've been seeing that therapist, right?"

Sandy nodded. "Pam told me. She saw that same woman when we were dating."

"Really? So you've told her about my issues?"

"Just the broad strokes. She asked who you were seeing."

"I won't go into what we've been doing 'cause I'd have never believed I could do half the stuff, but in some strange ways, it's helping. A lot. At least helping me to sleep better. Anyway, I really want to see Greta if only for a day. I don't want to wait till Labor Day or even later if her aunt begs her to stay."

"Go."

"What? Really? You're okay with this?"

"We'll manage."

"Are you sure?"

"Absolutely. Make your reservations and go."

"But who will fill in? Should I choose one of the guys and—"

"Me. I'll take over as manager."

Dumbfounded, Murph stared at his friend. "Really?"

Sandy grinned. "Why? You don't think I can do it?"

"Course not. I mean, I know you can, it's just—"

"This is why I'm determined to hire a comanager. Hopefully now you'll be on board with the idea?"

The two men had been squabbling about the second manager all month with Murph strongly resisting the idea of sharing his job. He shrugged. "Guess I'll have to be, won't I? I was thinking next Sunday."

"So you have a candidate in mind?"

"No, I mean for the California trip. I'd fly out Sunday and come home Tuesday."

"Take the weekend. We'll be fine. Maisie and her mom are going somewhere, so I won't have her. Perfect timing."

"I'll get everything organized. You know, leave lists, order everything, and—"

Sandy stood, brushing his long dark hair from his forehead in the swashbuckler move that made women swoon. In fact, there were already as many groupies that came to Field and Fire to catch a glimpse of the handsome owner as there had been at Sandy's. "Make your flights and don't worry about us. Everything'll be fine."

Murph hopped up, grinning. "Thanks, man. I owe you big time."

"You sure do, and you'll be paying when you return. Now stand aside. I've got a camper to walk over to the farm."

When his boss disappeared, Murph sat at the computer and punched in the airline website URL. *You're really doing this, buddy! Hope it's the right thing.*

"Why did I say yes?" Greta said, pacing back and forth on Sarah's back porch.

"Because you're in love with him and want to give him one more chance."

Greta turned and stared at her aunt, who lounged in a wicker settee, its comfortable floral cushions in perfect harmony with their surroundings. Sarah's backyard gardens were a riot of tangled, wild color.

"In love? Where did that come from?" she said.

"Oh, come on, girl, I wasn't born yesterday. You've been mooning around here for weeks." Just a wisp of a thing, Sarah's frail petite frame looked as if the slightest breeze would blow her away. Her salt-and-pepper hair fell in a thick braid down her back, violet eyes the mirror image of her niece's. She favored jeans and peasant blouses, and today was no exception. Bright, intricate embroidery embellished her well-worn top.

Greta stopped pacing and flopped down on an upholstered wicker chair. "Well, I don't know how I feel about Murphy O'Neill, but I'm certainly not ready to say I love him." *Liar, liar, pants on fire!*

Sarah sipped her iced tea. "It'll be fun to have a visitor. Did you send him the information about the Periwinkle?"

"Yes, and he's booked a room."

"Good, he'll be a short stroll away, although I still don't understand why we couldn't have just hosted him here. There's plenty of room."

Greta raised her hands. "Too awkward. Now, give me the grocery list, and I'll head into town." Before the market, she intended to visit a couple of clothing shops and pick up a few new things for her time with Murph.

Several hours later, she unpacked the groceries, then laid out her new clothes on the bed—a new summer dress, several tops, and two pairs of capris. Nothing fancy, but it was nice to have something new. *Maybe the clothes will distract my attention and prevent any swooning should he get too near!*

CHAPTER 24

After a long flight, Murph's plane landed in the pouring rain at San Jose Airport Saturday afternoon. After picking up his rental car, he punched the address of the Periwinkle B and B into Google Maps and headed southwest. It was four thirty and the sun was out as he pulled up and parked alongside the colorful Victorian at the end of a dead-end street of colorful cottages of all shapes and sizes. *This must be Oz*, he thought as he grabbed his bag, stepped out into the moist humid air, and headed up the porch steps. The inner door was open, so he pushed open the screen door and called, "Hello?"

Immediately, a tall middle-aged woman with ramrod-straight posture and a remarkable head of thick red hair appeared. She was barefoot, in jeans and a paint-spattered shirt. "Welcome! You must be Mr. O'Neill."

"Murph. Hello."

"I'm Peggy Periwinkle. Pleased to have you. Come in, come in! Sarah Pullman's one of my closest friends."

"I'm looking forward to meeting her. I'm here to see her niece."

"I heard. I hope you don't make a mess of things, young man. That Greta's a peach, and she's been a lifesaver for her aunt this summer."

"So I understand."

"Let me show you your room. It's up the stairs to the left. Nice view of the ocean. The ocean breezes'll get rid of that goop in an hour or so, but there's AC if you need it."

He followed her up to a light-filled, airy space with a queen-size bed, white-painted furnishings and seashells, mermaids and beach knickknacks on every surface. "What do you think?" Peggy asked, gesturing at the space.

"Very nice," he said, smiling.

"Bathroom's there, and there's a small balcony."

"Thanks, Ms. Periwinkle."

"Peggy, please. You may be a young fella, but I'm not that old. Here are your keys to the outside door and this room. You're welcome to grab cold drinks, snacks, or food from the kitchen anytime. Breakfast is from seven to nine. Coffee, tea, and sherry are always available in the parlor. I think that's it. Give a holler if I can help."

"Thanks," he said as Peggy Periwinkle closed the door behind her.

Murph sat on the bed, pulled out his phone, and punched in Greta's number. She answered on the second ring. "Hello?"

"Hey, it's me."

"Where are you?"

"In my room at the Periwinkle."

"Oh, my goodness, you're here, then!"

"Yup."

"I made a reservation for dinner at seven thirty tonight. Do you think you'd be up for that?"

"Of course. I just need a shower, and I'm good to go."

"The restaurant's a five-minute walk from here. We're only two minutes down the street from you, by the way."

"Wow, that's convenient."

"My aunt wants to meet you. Would that be okay?"

"That'd be great."

"Why don't you plan to come here around six. We can have a drink with Sarah, then walk around the corner."

"I'll be there."

"We're at number four, white cottage with blue shutters. Peggy can direct you."

"I'm sure I'll find it. Thanks."

"Well then, I'll see you in a bit. I can't believe you're here actually."

"Me neither. Is this restaurant fancy, by the way?"

"No, very casual. Most things are in Carmel."

"Okay, then. See you at six," he said, and they hung up.

That went pretty well, Murph mused as he unpacked and headed in for a shower.

❧

AFTER A VERY SHORT WALK, HE KNOCKED AT THE COTTAGE DOOR promptly at six. The smell of jasmine in the air was almost intoxicating as he waited. Just as Peggy promised, the humidity had lifted and the breeze was cool and dry. Then Greta was there, opening the door. "Hello."

"Hey," he said, embracing her awkwardly as he stepped in.

"Well, don't stand around out there," a voice called from the other end of the room. "Come on back so I can get a look at you."

He gazed at Greta, and she whispered, "Ignore the attitude. That's just Sarah."

He followed her to a wide screened-in porch at the rear of the house overlooking lush, beautiful gardens. A tiny woman reclined on a settee, a large goblet of white wine in her hand. Murph could see the family resemblance. Sarah Pullman was frail, but possessed a delicate, luminous beauty like her niece.

"Well, well," she said. "I finally get to meet the elusive Mr. O'Neill who's broken my niece's heart."

"Sarah!" Greta cried, gazing over at Murph as he stepped forward to shake the older woman's outstretched hand.

"Pleased to meet you, Ms. Pullman. Please call me Murph."

"Sarah, honey, and I'll reserve judgment about the Murph business. Sit. What can my niece get you to drink?"

"I'd love a beer, if you have one," he said, taking the nearest chair opposite his hostess.

Greta returned shortly with a small glass of white wine for herself and his beer in a frosted mug.

"Now then, we have our drinks. How are we going to proceed?" the older woman asked, a mischievous smile playing across her pretty face.

Greta sat in a matching chair next to Murph. "We're going to talk about Carmel-by-the-Sea, Murph's flight, or any other mundane topic. We will not be giving anyone the third degree."

They spent an enjoyable hour conversing about many topics. Finally, Greta stood. "Time to go, I'm afraid." She looked over at Murph. "If you'll excuse me a minute?"

She returned several minutes later carrying a tray with a sandwich and salad as well as a small dish of what looked like pudding. She set it down on the coffee table in front of her aunt.

"Thanks baby, but I think I'll eat inside and watch the news," Sarah said. "I'm sure Murph will give me his strong arm to escort me inside while you follow with the tray?"

"Of course," Greta said, smiling at him as he stooped to help Sarah to her feet.

CHAPTER 25

They walked a minute or two in silence before Greta said, "I'm sorry if Aunt Sarah was too much. She's always been a live wire. The polar opposite of my mom, her sister."

Murph met her eyes. "I thought she was great. You're lucky."

"Yes, I 'spose I am. She's tough, though. Tougher than you saw tonight. She can be very moody. Of course, this time with her is precious, but I do miss home."

"Your little Daisy's doing fine."

"Oh?"

"I stop by and see her when I know Lydia's at work."

"That's nice of you."

He smiled. "I've gotten kind of attached to her."

Greta grinned in spite of herself. *Are we talking about goats or people?* "Oh? What's Lydia doing for work?"

"She's waitressing at Field and Fire a couple of days a week, and she works for Kitty Bannister doing landscaping. Apparently, she wants to go to horticultural school."

"Wow, she's really settling in, isn't she?"

"She and the Wolfman are pretty tight."

Greta smiled. "So I hear."

"Thanks for letting me come."

"To be honest, I wasn't sure it was a good idea, but I'm glad you're here."

"Me too."

"Well, here it is. Funky little place."

Murph looked up and read the sign for The Back Eddy. "Looks like my kind of place."

"That's why I chose it," she said, meeting his eyes.

"God, I've missed you, Greta. It's literally tearing me apart."

"You're not alone... I mean in the missing part," she said, glimpsing the strong feelings in his eyes as well as the realization that her body was on fire being this close to him.

Without warning, he pulled her into his arms, capturing her lips in a deep, lingering kiss that left no doubt about how much he'd missed her or wanted her now. Greta returned the kiss, her tongue loving the feel of him, his arms, his woodsy scent full of spices and the sea. She loved every inch of him. As people passed by, she came to her senses and pushed back. "We'd better go in," she said, breathlessly, wondering if she'd be able to walk.

"Probably smart," he whispered, his deep voice husky.

THE BACK EDDY SPECIALIZED IN WHAT THEY DESCRIBED AS CALIFORNIA seafood. "What's good?" Murph asked, gazing at the extensive menu.

"Everything. I usually get the half bowl of cioppino. It's plenty for me, and I even take some home. They use red snapper, which I love, and langostino, clawless lobsters."

"Sounds good."

The waitress appeared. She introduced herself as Nancy. In shorts and a white T-shirt emblazoned with the company name and logo, she looked to be in her early thirties. Murph ordered a beer, and Greta a white wine. "So how have you been?" he asked as Nancy headed for the bar.

"Good. Spending time with Sarah has been fun, exasperating at times, and a nice change of pace after a hectic school year. *Not to mention a passionate love affair that broke my heart.* I'm glad to be able to help her, but I'd be lying if I said I didn't miss home and Daisy." *And you.*

"I get that."

"How about you? You mentioned you'd been seeing a therapist. Has it been helpful?"

Murph gulped as the color drained from his face. "I think so. Yes. It's not easy, but it's beginning to give me some peace. We'll see. I'm happy to deal with the rough spots if it helps."

"Of course it will."

Nancy returned with their drinks. "What can I get you folks?" Her curly blonde hair was tied in a ponytail, a pencil sticking out of one side, which she extracted and poised over her order pad. They both ordered the cioppino, Greta a half, Murph a whole.

When she departed, he said, "What I meant to say is, it's worth it if it helps here, with you and me."

"I hope it helps us, Murph, but mostly I hope it supports you. No matter what happens with us, you deserve that."

As he met her gaze, Murph's eyes reflected sadness and what looked like anxiety. "I'm not sure I could adequately explain what I've been doing with Carroll. Sometimes we talk, and others... I guess you'd call it experiential with a little cognitive based therapy thrown in. We've chanted and sang in a language I still can't understand."

Greta smiled. "I've heard really good things about Carroll's work."

He shrugged. "Truthfully this," he said waving his hand between them, "is still feeling scary. Maybe friends for now?"

"Was that what you call a friendly kiss outside?"

"Sorry. Momentary slip."

Greta wasn't sure how she felt about being part of a momentary slip, so she asked, "So can you explain to me how that will work?"

Somehow, her words, or maybe the whole discussion, suddenly created an awkwardness between them and they fell silent for a few minutes. Once Nancy set their meals in front of them—steaming bowls of fish stew, a basket of garlic bread, and a large empty bowl for shells—Greta suggested they talk about Horseshoe Crab Cove Field and Fire and what was going on at home. These neutral topics carried them through dinner. Both too full for dessert, Murph paid the bill, and they headed out.

"I wish you'd let me pay half," she said as they strolled along the quiet street.

"Are you kidding? It's the least I can do. Besides, Sandy pays me a ridiculous salary, four times what I'm worth."

"I've heard he's a generous boss."

"That's an understatement."

"So how long are you here?"

"Just tomorrow, then I fly home early the next morning."

"Would you like to do something? Beach, sightseeing, whatever. I don't guess you're a shopper?"

"Anything's great. You're right, I'm not much of a shopper. Kind of a bull in a china shop, but if that's what you'd like, I'll keep my elbows in."

Greta laughed. "I'm not crazy about shopping either. If I can buy it online, I do."

"Well, you know the area. Why don't you plan something you'd like to do with a friend." Their arms brushed against each other, sending shockwaves of sensation through him.

"I'll phone in the morning. Maybe after Peggy's breakfast? She'd be so offended if you didn't eat her breakfast."

"Great."

"Sarah asked if you'd come to dinner tomorrow night. We can get takeout. Do you mind?"

"Of course not."

They stood on the cottage's front porch, and he leaned forward, kissing her cheek. "This was nice."

"Yes," she said, hugging him briefly even as she longed to throw herself into his strong arms and never let go. "Night."

"Night."

Door closed behind her, Greta took a deep breath. She wasn't sure how she felt about the evening. Aside from their one moment of passion, it had felt a bit forced and stilted. *How will we ever get through tomorrow?*

CHAPTER 26

How the hell am I going to spend a whole day with Greta and pretend we're just friends? Murph thought as he walked the short distance to Sarah's cottage Sunday morning at nine, stuffed after Peggy's enormous breakfast. *Friends? That's a laugh when every time I see her I want to take her in my arms and kiss her silly and a whole lot more!*

Their dinner had been really awkward, each of them trying so hard to be light and friendly rather than expressing what they really felt. The work with Carroll and now this visit were exhausting, admitting he loved her still too scary. "You can only pretend it away for so long," Carroll had said at their last appointment. "Pretense becomes more destructive than truth in affairs of the heart." *The truth? When have I ever told the truth except a few rare moments with my best friend?* Speaking candidly to Sandy had always felt safe.

Greta opened the door, a big smile on her face. "Good morning! How was breakfast?"

"Filling," he said, returning her smile. She looked lovely in a pale pink linen top, gray capris, and sandals. Delicate and waiflike. Murph's protective instincts had kicked in from the moment he saw her chasing that silly little goat.

"Big breakfast?"

"Yup, and I was still full from last night, but Peggy wouldn't take no for an answer. I was also the only diner."

Greta laughed her deep, throaty laugh. "Maybe a light lunch at the beach?"

"Sounds good."

"Let me grab my bag, and we can head out. I forgot to ask, can we take your car? Aunt Sarah took hers."

"Of course."

They strolled back to the Periwinkle and hopped into his rental, a small SUV. He started the car, then turned to her. "Where to?"

"I was thinking since you've never been out here that we should take a drive down the coast. It's really beautiful. If you're up for it, San Simeon is two hours away. The Hearst Castle is there, and I've always wanted to go."

"You're the boss."

Greta grinned. "I was hoping you'd say that. Don't go yet. Let me tell you the different tours, and we can decide which we want to do. I think we might be able to squeeze in two if they have openings."

She pulled up the castle website on her phone and rattled off their options. They chose the main tour and a tour of the grounds, then she called and reserved both. "Okay, all set. I'm sure we can find a place to grab lunch somewhere along the way or in San Simeon."

She directed him to Route One, the iconic Pacific Coast Highway, which had dramatic views of the Pacific most of its length. Between oohing and aahing at the rugged coastline, they chatted about everyday topics, steering clear of Murph and his issues, or their relationship.

The tours of San Simeon proved to be a perfect way to spend a friendly day, leaving little time for private conversation. The vast estate of William Randolph Hearst was, indeed, one-of-a-kind, with so much history, incredible artwork and architecture, and echoes of Hollywood's golden age everywhere. They got takeout from a small roadside restaurant and enjoyed their lunch seated in the gardens in between tours.

"This is pretty amazing," he said. "I was thinking it'd be like Newport and the mansions, but it's so much cooler."

Greta gave him a look. "I take it you're not a fan of the Breakers?"

He shrugged. "What can I say? I'm a guy. If you've seen one mansion, you've seen 'em all, but this is different."

She nodded. "In scale, size, and history. Outrageous, isn't it?"

THEY WERE QUIET ON THE RIDE BACK, SO MUCH SO THAT GRETA FELL asleep, leaning over, almost touching his shoulder. Murph smiled gazing at her lush, beautiful lips, her long lashes hiding brilliant violet eyes, and her pale peach cheeks, flushed and slightly tanned from their day in the sun. She was the most beautiful woman he'd ever seen, inside and out, and he couldn't imagine a life without her in it. As they neared Carmel-by-the-Sea, he watched for what he thought was the exit and turned off the Coast Highway only to find himself in strange territory. He took out his phone and pulled up Google Maps. The Periwinkle was the last destination he had searched, so he pushed "Go," and the GPS began to speak to him.

The sound woke Greta, who stirred and sat up, disoriented for a minute. "Oh, goodness, I didn't mean to conk out on you. Where are we?"

Murph laughed. "You tell me. According to Google Maps, about eight miles from home. I'm happy to shut off the robotic voice and have you direct me."

"Oh, Murph, I'm sorry. Some date I am. I mean, not date. Friend or whatever."

"No problem. I was happy to enjoy the scenery outside and inside."

Greta felt her face turn beet red. *Inside indeed!* Truth was, she hadn't been sleeping ever since Murph called and asked to visit, and the lack of sleep had caught up with her. "Ha-ha, take a left at the next light."

As they pulled up to Sarah's, he asked, "Okay to park here, or should I drop you and park the car at the Periwinkle?"

"This is fine. Just pull into the driveway behind Sarah's car."

As he parked and she made a move to alight, he reached over and took her arm. "Wait, Greta."

"Is something wrong?"

"No, everything's right. I just wanted to say thanks for today. It felt... I don't know...just normal after the past month. It was fun too. There's nowhere I'd rather be than with you."

"Me too. And thank you for the castle. I've always wanted to go to San Simeon, and we've never gotten down there before. I know it's not your thing, so I'm really grateful to you for taking me."

He reached up to caress her cheek. "Anywhere we go is my thing if I'm with you."

"Hmm, I can think of a few places where you'd probably draw the line." She put her hand over his and gently brought both down. "Better hop out, or our friends thing might be challenged."

"Got that right," he said.

CHAPTER 27

Dinner with Aunt Sarah proved lively and fun. They'd ordered enough Chinese food to feed an army and ate at the table on the back porch.

"This might be the best Chinese food I've ever had," Murph said.

"Jade's is kind of legendary," Greta said, then popped a dumpling into her mouth.

"So do you really have to leave us tomorrow, dear?" Sarah asked.

"'Fraid so. My boss'd kill me if I stayed longer. We're short-staffed at the moment, and the restaurant's busier than we expected for its first month."

"Lucky you."

"Yeah. My boss is phenomenal. Anything he touches turns to gold. Every one of his businesses has been super successful, and he's always brought me along with him."

"He should make you a partner at this point," Greta said.

"His money, his business. Besides, my salary is more than generous, and I like what I'm doing. Being an owner doesn't interest me. Too many headaches. If I weren't with Sandy, I'd probably be a farmer."

"Somehow I don't see you on the farm," Sarah said, eyeing him thoughtfully.

Murph shrugged. "Who knows. That's where I grew up. On a farm and in a bar."

"So what about you and my niece? I know you care for her."

"Sarah!" Greta said, her voice sharper than she intended. "Don't answer that, Murph."

He chuckled, setting down his chopsticks. "You have every right to ask, and I wish I could give you a clear answer. I'm in the middle of something right now. It wouldn't be fair to Greta."

"Isn't that up to her to decide?" the older woman said.

Greta stood up. "That's enough. I'll clear these later. I'm going to walk Murph back to the Periwinkle."

"It's okay, Greta, really," he said.

"No, it isn't." With that, she turned and headed into the house.

Murph turned back to his hostess. "I guess this is goodbye. My flight's at five thirty in the morning. Thanks for dinner."

Sarah waved, and Murph suddenly realized she was drunk. Very drunk. "Don't pay me any mind, sweetie. Safe trip back."

She reached up as he stooped to hug her. "Thanks, Ms. Pullman."

HE FOUND GRETA SITTING ON THE FRONT STEPS, FUMING. "HEY, YOU okay?"

"No. I'm mad. I love my aunt, but her drinking has gotten much worse. I've committed to stay till the end of August, but I'm not sure I'll make it. I should have known when she took the car today it was so she could load up at all the liquor stores on her circuit."

Murph sat beside her, draping his arm around her shoulder. "I'm sorry. We went through this with my dad. It sucks."

"Sarah's drinking worried my mom for years. Every time she'd hang up the phone, she be in tears. There was nothing she could do from so far away. When she visited, Sarah could keep things under control, but the minute she left, boom, right off the wagon again. Ever since my Uncle Ralph died, it's been like this, although I suspect Sarah's been an alcoholic since her teens."

"What about her kids? Can't they intervene?"

"Her son, Ralph Junior, has tried. She's pretty good at hiding things when he's around, and she's been great for most of this visit. I've been hiding or pouring out all her liquor. In true alcoholic fashion, she never asks where it is. Just goes out and buys more."

He pulled her closer, kissing the top of her head. "I'm sorry. Is there anything I can do?"

It felt so good to be in his arms, drawing comfort from his strength and warmth. *If only I could stay here forever*, she thought as she stood, moving out of his embrace. "No, I'll get her under control tomorrow. Uncover her stash. Come on, let's get you back to the Periwinkle. It's late, and you've got an early flight."

They walked side by side to the front steps of the B and B. Murph turned to her. "This isn't very gallant, the woman walking the man home. Should be the reverse."

"Home turf," she said. "Besides, it gives me a few more minutes to cool off and be with you."

"Shit, Greta, I've made such a mess out of us."

"No, you haven't. You're working stuff out. Important stuff."

"Did I drive you out of town for the summer?"

She shook her head. "No, I'd have come anyway. For my mom's sake and Sarah's. I love my aunt."

"Of course you do," he said, drawing her close, hands on her waist as he kissed her forehead. "Come back home soon."

"Give me something to keep me going?" She stood on tiptoes and found his lips.

He drew her to him, returning the kiss.

Every fiber of her being wanted to follow him into the B and B and have wild, unbridled sex in one of Peggy's comfy beds, but Greta pulled back as she felt him grow hard against her belly. "That'll have to keep me, my friend," she whispered.

"I guess so. Take care of yourself."

"You too."

As he turned away and walked up the porch steps, Greta felt like her heart had been ripped from her chest. He waved at the door, then stood watching to make sure she got safely home. She waved from Sarah's porch, then went in, steeling herself for what awaited her.

"Bye, my darling," she whispered to the night air. "I love you."

CHAPTER 28

As his plane taxied to the runway the next morning, Murph wondered whether it had been the right decision to come to California. On the one hand they were talking, on the other hand did the visit give them false hope that would be dashed away when she returned? As the plane lifted off, he reclined his seat and closed his eyes. *Whatever happens it was worth it. It was beyond amazing to hold her in my arms, to kiss her again, all of it, even drunken Aunt Sarah.*

Greta had not spoken to her aunt the previous evening after saying goodbye to Murph. Sarah was passed out on her wicker settee, so she covered her with blanket, cleared the table, washed up, and went to bed. This morning, Sarah was still asleep on the porch, so Greta grabbed her bag and headed out to the bakery on the corner. When she returned, she boiled eggs and made up a tray for her aunt with her soft boiled eggs and the soldiers she adored, fresh scones and coffee. When she stepped onto the porch with the tray, Sarah was sitting up.

"Thanks dearie," she said as her niece set the tray on the table in front of her.

Greta nodded, turning to go.

"I made a mess of things last night, didn't I?"

"Of yourself, yes," Greta said from the doorway.

"I'm sorry, sweetie. Your Murph seems like a lovely man. I hope I didn't scare him off."

"He's seen it before. His dad's an alcoholic." She hadn't meant to sound so harsh. Feeling guilty, she came back onto the porch and took the chair next to her aunt.

Sarah raised an eyebrow and huffed, "Well, I guess that put me in my place."

"I don't mean to be cruel, Sarah, but you are an alcoholic. Problem drinker. Substance abuser. Whatever label you want to put on it."

"I don't drink every day."

"No, but when you do, it's a problem because you don't stop."

"Is this the social worker talking?"

"No, it's your niece who loves you and is concerned about you. The daughter of your sister who cried herself to sleep many nights after one of your drunken phone calls."

"I never meant to hurt your mama."

"I know. Drunks never do mean to hurt anyone. They use the bottle as an excuse to do any mean, nasty, stupid thing they want. Then they walk away, taking no responsibility for their actions."

"Oh, honey, you *are* angry."

"Not about last night. I'm angry because you're wasting your life and hurting yourself and others. What about Ralph Junior and your grandkids? Have you ever wondered why Hattie never wants to come here or bring the kids?"

"Fine. I'll stop."

"Not without help you won't."

"What kind of help?"

"Well, I'd suggest a good therapist and also you should find a local AA group and go to meetings. I'll go with you if you want."

Sarah shrugged, taking one of the sticks of toast, her soldier, and dipping it into the soft boiled egg yolk. "I'll think about it. Thanks for breakfast."

Greta rose, went back to the kitchen, and poured a second mug of coffee. She sat in the sunny breakfast alcove munching on a ginger scone and reading the Sunday paper. She found herself thinking of Murph, her loving community and Daisy, and counting the days till she could fly home.

Several days later, Sarah announced that she would like to try AA. For the remainder of her stay, Greta had a regular activity most evenings. She would drive Sarah to a local church and sit in the car or on a bench outside while she attended a meeting with all her "new friends." Greta had accompanied her to the first evening, but, wanting to give everyone, including her aunt, their privacy, she told Sarah it would be best for her to wait outside.

Those evenings sitting by herself, sometimes reading, other times watching the sunset, proved to be nurturing, reflective moments for Greta. Moments where she examined what she wanted next in life. Was it the messiness of a relationship with all its joys and ups and downs? Or did solitude suit her best?

One evening, she sat watching a glorious California sunset. The pastor of the church, with whom she now had a nodding familiarity after seeing each other each evening, approached. "May I?" he asked, indicating the bench beside her.

"Of course," Greta said, startled by his request.

He gazed out at the sunset. "You never get tired of this."

"No."

About her age, the minister reminded her of Ichabod Crane, with his long gangly legs, crook nose, and dark garb. His eyes were kind and full of light when they met hers. "You have a loved one in the meeting?"

Greta nodded.

"I hope it's proving helpful."

"Time will tell, I guess."

"It's a long journey."

"So I understand."

"We also host an Al-Anon meeting on Saturdays for family members."

"Thank you, but I'm returning home to Massachusetts next week. I'm not her usual caregiver, just a summer stand-in."

"What will she do when you're gone?"

"She has friends and a son, and now this meeting. She seems to like the other members and feels comfortable. Maybe some of the drinking has been because of loneliness?"

"It's a friendly meeting. We're also a friendly church, if she ever needs counsel or fellowship."

"Thank you. I'll tell her."

He reached in his pocket and handed her a business card. "For you and for your loved one. I'm John Collins."

"Thank you," she said, taking the card and slipping it into her bag.

"Good night, then," he said, and turned to go, walking away in the twilight.

CHAPTER 29

Life went into overdrive for Murph upon his return. Between his sessions with Carroll and Field and Fire, he was going from early morning until late at night. The third week of August, they completed interviews for the comanager position and offered the job to Aurora Lake, or Rori, a thirty-six-year-old former restaurant owner who wanted the "excitement of the food world, without the stress."

The minute the statuesque Rori, with her long auburn hair and air of friendly confidence, stepped through the front door, they knew they had their comanager. She greeted Sandy, Murph, and Meryl with firm handshakes, her luminous gray eyes taking in her surroundings and companions.

"What an amazing space! How lucky are you? Someone with extraordinary vision created this."

Murph pointed to his friend standing beside him. "That would be him. He's the genius designer, Meryl's the genius chef, and I'm the workhorse that does whatever they need."

She laughed. "I love that description. That's the job I'm seeking. A support person for geniuses."

"Okay, okay, enough with the geniuses," Sandy said, leading the way to a table with pitchers of iced tea, water, and glasses. "Let's sit down, Ms. Lake. We can tell you about the job, and you can tell us about you and whether you think you'd be a good fit."

Rori Lake, a Midwesterner, but most recently from Westerly, Rhode Island, impressed the team enough that Sandy phoned her a half hour after their conversation and offered her the job. Within a week, she'd found a rental, one of the cottages at the newly renovated Barnum's Ledge. Jack Faulkner, the project manager, gave her a good rate because she would be surrounded by construction for at least a year.

From day one, Rori and Murph had gotten along like two peas in a pod. She was an excellent listener and made it clear that she wanted to learn from him. The remarkable thing about Rori was her almost total lack of ego. "Been there, done that," she'd say if asked whether she'd rather do something a different way from her boss and coworkers. "If you think it's a good idea, I'm in. Once I get to know things, I'll be happy to give my two cents, if asked."

Late morning of her second week, they finished the ordering, and she and Murph headed over to the winery to meet with Wolfie. After putting in the wine order, Murph said he had to go into town on a bunch of errands and asked if she'd like to go with him and grab lunch. She took her own car because she needed to stop at home and also had errands of her own, and they met at the Crab Café on Main Street.

"Such a great day, and the Café's packed. Why don't we grab lunch and eat in the garden?" Murph suggested.

"Garden?"

"You'll see. Come on."

They picked up their food, and he led the way down Main Street to Laura's Community Garden.

"Wow," she said as they entered through the arbor, now covered with climbing roses. "I've been so focused on Field and Fire and my little cottage that I haven't come this way. I didn't even know this was here."

"I'm surprised. It's the brainchild of our boss's wife."

"Pam?"

"Yup. Laura was her mom. Died over twenty years ago."

"I saw the bench on the ridge when the Morgans had me to dinner last week, but they didn't mention the garden. This is very cool. How does one get a plot?"

"I think you put your name in, and they have a lottery when plots open up. They're always expanding. If you were staying on over at Barnum's Ledge, I'd say ask Jack Faulkner to put something like this in over there. He's open to anything."

They sat on a bench in the shade at the far end of the garden, watching a half dozen gardeners go about the work of weeding, watering, and picking. "Hmm, what I'd rather work on is him selling me my cottage. I absolutely love it there, which is probably the reason that I've yet to explore this incredible village. I haven't been able to tear myself away from decorating my little home."

Murph grinned. "You're lucky. Barnum's Ledge is a very cool spot."

They ate while chatting about work and dividing jobs for the evening ahead. Finally, Rori stood, brushing crumbs off her beige capris and sleeveless jersey top. Murph had to admit, his new partner was gorgeous, her slim arms toned with a hint of a tan. She didn't hold a candle to Greta—no woman ever could—but Rori Lake was beautiful.

As they walked out of the garden, he asked, "Hey, why doesn't a person like you have a boyfriend, or are you hiding him somewhere?"

"Taking a break, after a miserable breakup. One of the reasons I wanted to move. My ex-fiancé and I owned a really successful restaurant in Westerly. Two years of that and we were done. His many infidelities didn't help matters. And that, my dear Mr. O'Neill, is all you'll ever hear about that sad story. How about you? Where's your Ms. Right? Someone told me you had a girlfriend. Is *she* hiding somewhere?"

"California, although we've scaled back our relationship to a friendship."

"Uh-oh."

"My issue, not hers. Greta's perfect."

"Too bad she's in California. How'd that happen?"

"She's been taking care of her aunt. She'll be home in a week or two."

"Can't wait to meet her. Something tells me there's more than friendship, judging by the way you look when talking about her."

He grinned. "Time will tell. I gotta run. See you back at the restaurant around four?"

"Perfect."

CHAPTER 30

Murph stopped in at the hardware store and then headed down the coast to Lindels. A few of the plantings around the restaurant had died, and their landscaper, Kitty Bannister, was away. He intended to buy a few replacement bushes and have them planted before the dinner crowd arrived. After making his selections and paying, he was loading his truck when he heard a voice call, "Hey, Murph! Long time no see."

It was his old girlfriend, Sadie Riley. Sadie worked for one of the Darn Yarners, Hope Childs at the Cove Yoga Center. In fact, she was by far the center's most popular yoga teacher. "Hey, Sadie," he said, depositing the last pot in his truck bed and closing the tailgate.

A beautiful flowering plant in shades of pink and coral in her arms, she approached, setting the plant on the ground. "How are you?" she asked, coming to hug him.

"Good, great. Restaurant's a success, but what isn't in Sandy's hands?"

"And yours."

He grinned. "I do what I'm told."

"And a whole lot more, I'm sure," she said, smiling. Blonde, lithe, and petite, Sadie looked lovely in yoga tights and a body-hugging top.

"I drove by you on Main Street before. Is that gorgeous redhead a new girlfriend?"

He laughed. "You mean Rori? No, she's my comanager at Field and Fire. Just came onboard a couple of weeks ago."

"Well, you looked pretty chummy."

"We are. As comanagers. Work chums only."

"Uh-huh."

"Hey, Sadie, have you got a minute?"

"For you? Sure."

"Wanna grab a lemonade and sit?" He gestured to the Del's Lemonade truck parked near a row of benches Lindels provided customers in case they wanted to relax before or after their shopping.

"Sure."

Once they sat side by side, small frozen lemonades in hand, she turned to him. "So what's on your mind?"

"How are you doing?" he asked.

"I'm great, never better."

Why don't I believe you? he thought, watching her, observing a sadness playing around her eyes. "I'm sorry if I hurt you, Sadie."

"Where's this coming from?"

"I've been doing some work... I mean some therapy. Trying to resolve everything that happened with Aislan. I think her death has made it impossible for me to get close to women, or at least to stay close."

"That's a good thing, isn't it? The therapy?"

"Yes. What I wanted to ask is... I mean, when we were together, did you think I was really messed up? That I needed therapy?"

"I'm not sure what you want me to say, Murph. Yes, I was hurt when you broke things off, and I'd be lying if I said I don't still have feelings for you, but I never saw you as screwed-up. Just the opposite. You always seemed like a solid, steady, salt-of-the-earth guy."

He grinned, shaking his head. "I guess looks can be deceiving, can't they?"

"Maybe. Why are you asking now?"

"There is someone... She's—"

"Greta Jeffers."

"You know about Greta?"

"Small town, remember? Isn't she away for the summer?"

"Yup. Gets back next week."

"And how are things with you two, if I might be nosey?"

"We've decided to be friends as I work through my past."

"And how's that working out?"

"It has its ups and downs."

"If she's the one, I'm happy for you."

"Thanks."

"Listen, I've got to get this plant to the studio. Hope's having an open house, and she sent me for a few decorations."

"Yeah, I gotta go too. Thanks Sadie."

"No problem," she said, hugging him again.

Before she turned away to grab her plant, he saw her eyes were rimmed with tears.

He spent an hour putting in the new bushes, trying to clear his head for the evening ahead. He felt guilty thinking about Sadie, but there was no help for it. Their relationship was in the past, and Sadie was not Greta. He had never been in love with Sadie. He knew that for certain. He also knew that he was in love with Greta. Madly, deeply, hopelessly in love.

CHAPTER 31

As Kevin Averill pulled into her driveway, it was all Greta could do not to burst into tears. *Home.* It felt so good. After paying Kevin and rolling her bags into the front hall, she ran through the house and threw open the slider. At first, there was no sign of Daisy, then the little goat peeked out of the shed, ears cocked. When she spied her mistress, she bleated and began running at full tilt across the lawn.

"Daisy!" Greta cried as they rolled in the grass. "My sweet girl! You've gotten so big!"

The goat licked her cheeks and bleated softly, rubbing against her before settling in her arms. As she cradled her pet, Greta gazed around the yard. Although the gardens looked a bit shaggy, they were still in full bloom, a riot of color particularly along the north wall. "So you haven't eaten everything up," she said, ruffling Daisy's fur.

Finally, she hopped to her feet and headed into the house to unpack, the kid at her heels. She went through every room, breathing in gratitude to be home and safe. It had been so hard to be away from home. The ups and downs of life with Sarah had taken their toll. She had left her aunt in a good place. Her son Ralph was coming for a short visit and Sarah was fully mobile again. She actually looked forward to her evenings at AA. It had become her social life. She usually attended at least five meetings a week and had made a number of new friends. When Greta had said goodbye, she felt at peace. They had made a plan for Sarah to come to Horseshoe Crab Cove for Thanksgiving, so she knew she'd be seeing her soon.

Lyddie had moved out of the cottage that morning and left it spotless. After unpacking, Greta headed outside to garden for a few hours, then realized she'd better make a grocery run as there was not much food in the house. After a trip to the market and local farm stand, she came home laden with bags and boxes. Everywhere she'd gone, talk centered around an upcoming storm, which was still far to the south, but as it moved up the coast, it was expected to reach hurricane force in the next twenty-four to forty-eight hours. Greta had only experienced one powerful hurricane in her life, and she wasn't sure what measures to take. As she unpacked groceries, she flipped on the radio to listen to the weather report.

She poured a glass of wine and padded into the study to relax. She had just sat down when her cell phone rang. It was Pam inviting her to have dinner with herself and her sisters at Field and Fire the following evening. Greta accepted immediately. Only after she'd hung up did she think about how it would be seeing Murph. Their correspondence had been sporadic at best. A few texts and several brief phone calls. Overwhelmed and busy, he always seemed eager to get off the phone and never once mentioned how the therapy with Carroll Ranglund was going.

With three new waitstaff beginning that night, Murph and Rori buzzed around the restaurant all Friday training, setting up and putting out fires as they prepped for a full house. There were no tables available. Walk-ins could eat at the bar, but even that was iffy as the beautiful space had already become a popular spot. Pam and a couple of helpers were freshening the flowers, and Meryl and her staff had been working since early morning.

They had hired a dessert chef, but he wasn't scheduled to arrive until the following week. All summer, they'd been serving a combination of Meryl's creations and desserts from Moon and Stars Bakery in town. Moon and Stars also supplied the thick, crusty artisan breads they served. Their desserts were "out of this world," according to Meryl, even though she ultimately agreed that they needed a full-time patisserie.

"Hey, Murph," Pam called as she cleaned up and gathered her flower buckets and tools.

"Hey," he said. "See you tonight!"

As his boss's wife disappeared out the side door, he thought about Greta. He knew she was back, but he'd been too busy and confused to call her. After almost two months of therapy, trauma work and occasional conversations with Father Joe, he had decided that he was irrevocably screwed up and that he and Greta should stay friends. *Not fair. I'll rip the Band-Aid off and let her get on with her life. If she's still willing to stay friends, that'd be great, but I won't blame her if she tells me to take a hike.*

"Earth to Murph," Rori said, throwing a damp tea towel at him. "Where are tonight's menus?"

"Oh, sorry," he said, grinning. "In the office. I'll grab 'em."

"We're gonna have to grab a beer some night soon so you can tell me all about it."

"You don't want to know," he said, waving over his shoulder as he headed to the office.

In a few short weeks, Rori and he had clicked. They worked really well together and their repartee was like a brother and sister. Despite all his arguments, Sandy had been right—he needed a comanager. Murph never would have believed it, but the restaurant was more intense than Sandy's had ever been. So much more to organize, manage, and orchestrate. As he walked through the beautiful spaces, he shook his head, sad that he couldn't share it all with Greta. *Maybe a friendly dinner someday in future, if she'll even speak to me?*

As he pushed open the office door, he nearly ran into his boss. "Hey, where's the fire?"

Sandy asked, eying his friend.

"Menus. Madame Rori needs them to stack in that fancy pile she loves to create."

"Customers love it too. You okay?

"Yeah, fine."

"I hear Greta's back."

"So I'm told."

"Have you spoken to her?"

"Nope."

Murph grabbed the stack of menus and started for the door, but his friend barred the way. "Are you going to?"

Murph shrugged. "Maybe soon. Didn't want to bother her till she was all settled back at home."

"Uh-huh," Sandy said, still blocking the door.

"Look, man, we're just friends. Friends don't keep in touch every frickin' second."

"Friends? Yeah, right."

"I don't want to talk about it." He tried to shove by, but Sandy grabbed hold of his arm.

"Well, just a heads-up so you're not caught off guard. She's coming to eat tonight with Pam and her sisters."

Murph's stomach flipped. "Great. Now can I please get by?"

"Only looking out for you, buddy," Sandy called as the door swung shut.

Well, I have to see her sometime, Murph thought, dropping the menus at the reception desk and heading into the bar to check on things there. *Might as well be tonight when there's no time for anything but hello and goodbye.*

CHAPTER 32

The four sisters arrived at Greta's a little after six. Their reservation at Field and Fire was for seven thirty, so they all piled out for drinks on the terrace. No one but Pam had met Daisy. Weezie, the youngest Morgan sister, immediately began rolling around on the grass with the tiny goat, heedless of her pretty off-white summer sheath.

Gail rolled her eyes, watching them. "Grass stains will go really well with that, sis."

The Morgan sisters were quite a crew, and Greta had never been with all four together. Ava, the eldest, with long chestnut-brown hair and deep blue eyes, wore a pretty embroidered top and flowing floral skirt. She and her husband, Dan, ran the research lab at the village fishery. Gail, the PR person for Morgan Enterprises and now Field and Fire, had short curly auburn hair and wore a simple summer dress in a sage green that brought out the color in her eyes, and Weezie, petite like Gail, had short dark hair cut in a stylish pixie and eyes that sparkled with mischief. Pam wore a simple blue summer dress, her strawberry-blonde hair swept back, silver earrings and necklace her only adornment. They were lovely, all four of them. At first, Greta felt a bit intimidated in their presence, but not for long. Each was warm and friendly in her own way, and soon, the only child of overprotective parents found herself feeling almost like a fifth Morgan sister.

After margueritas and a few appetizers, the group rose to head out. The wind had picked up, and a glance at the ocean revealed angry whitecaps. "Storm's coming," Weezie said, stooping to pet Daisy.

"Yeah, I think I'll lock Daisy inside the shed," Greta said. "I still don't trust her in the house alone."

After securing Daisy with food, water, and fresh hay, they departed shortly after seven. "Doesn't hurt to get there early, and we can take a cliff walk first," Pam said. "We might be okay until the storms reaches us. It's so beautiful out there at this time of night."

THE NIGHT WAS, INDEED, BEAUTIFUL, SO THEY DECIDED TO PARK AT THE farmhouse and walk from Morgan's Fire along the cliffs. When they arrived, the place was hopping. A tall, gorgeous woman greeted them as they entered. "Hi, Rori," Pam said. "I don't think you've met my sisters or Greta. Ladies, this is Rori Lake, the new comanager of Field and Fire. Rori, my sisters Ava, Gail and Weezie, and our dear friend Greta Jeffers."

As they all greeted each other, Greta thought the maître d was studying her in particular eying her from head to toe. It could have been her imagination, but she wondered if someone had told her about her relationship with Murph. With a flourish, Rori showed them to their table by the windows in the smaller south dining room.

"This best table in the house. You must know the owner," Rori said, winking at Pam.

Pam smiled up at her. "Thanks, Rori. This is perfect."

When the comanager disappeared, Weezie leaned over to her sister. "You mean that's who's working with Murph? Wowee!"

Pam glanced at Greta's face, then nodded. "Yup, that's Rori. She's working out really well and has helped Murph so much as comanager. Sandy says she's way overqualified for the job since she's owned restaurants and stuff, but he's thrilled to have her."

Greta tried to keep her expression neutral as they discussed Rori Lake, but it was near impossible. She was sure her cheeks were flushed and blotchy. *Beautiful, accomplished, and she's joined at the hip to the man I love. There, I've admitted it. I love the man who just wants to be friends and is probably in bed with his gorgeous comanager!*

"Hi, ladies," said a voice behind her. Lydia Faulkner smiled down at the group, her sandy-blonde hair pulled back in a bun. In the same black slacks and crisp white blouse as the other waitstaff, she held a small iPad in her hand. "Greta, hi! You're here too! So glad to have you home. Was everything okay at the house?"

"It was perfect. Thank you so much Lyddie. I'll settle up with you this week. Are you at your dad's now?"

"Yup, until I head back to my apartment next week. So excited. I was in a dorm last year, but a few of us got this great apartment right near campus. It's just off Thayer Street, so it's super convenient." Lyddie was about to begin her sophomore year at Brown.

"Not far from here either," Pam said, smiling up at her. Lyddie and their brother Wolfie had been dating all summer and from all reports were still a couple.

"Yeah, my dad's keyed. And I'll be close by for his wedding."

"That's right," Gail said. "It's this fall, isn't it?"

"October fifteenth. We're all really excited. We love Lolly and Maisie. Now, what can I get you ladies? Something to drink to start you off?"

They consulted and ordered two bottles of cabernet sauvignon, then Lyddie rattled off the specials and disappeared.

"She's such a sweetheart," Pam said. "They're sure going to miss her when she goes."

"So what have you all heard about the storm?" Ava asked. "We've locked down everything we can at the lab. Last hurricane destroyed all the docks and several buildings, but at least the lab isn't right on the river."

"Oh, dear," Greta said. "I haven't been listening to the weather. I'm not very protected if the storm hits at high tide."

They chatted about the hurricane and village gossip until Lyddie returned with the wine in two silver buckets. After pouring it, she stepped back and asked if they were ready to order.

"Absolutely! I'm starved," Weezie said.

They all ordered different dishes—a hot seafood tower, grilled sea bass, swordfish pastrami, and mussels with arancini—and told Lyddie to bring serving spoons as they wanted to share family-style.

"Great idea. The fish dishes you ordered have been receiving raves, especially the sea bass. I'll bring some sticky rice and lots of bread. Trust me, you'll want them for the mussels. How about appetizers?"

"I think we're all set except for Weezie's chowder," Pam said. "But we'd love some bread now."

"Coming right up," Lyddie said, turning as one of the young waiters set baskets of warm crusty bread, butter, and flavored olive oils on the table.

"You girls are going to be sorry," Weezie said as they passed the bread baskets. "Meryl's chowder is supposed to be the best in the world."

Ava tipped her wineglass at her sister. "That's why we'll all be sampling yours."

CHAPTER 33

Murph spied Greta the moment she stepped into the restaurant. She was wearing the same sexy dress she'd worn for their dinner in California. It was all he could do to keep his mind on the job as Rori ushered them to their table. Fortunately, he was overseeing the bar tonight, so temptation would be two rooms away. *Friends, what a joke.*

"Hey, partner, where are you?" Rori asked, passing him as she headed back to the front desk. "Yes, she's here. Yes, she's beautiful, and yes, you should go over and say hi. Welcome her home and all."

"Mind your own business," he said, turning toward the bar.

"I am," she called. "The business of keeping this place on track with a lovestruck partner."

"Ha-ha," he mumbled. *Did everyone know his business?*

Halfway through dinner, Greta looked up to see the comanagers chatting at the doorway to their dining room. *They look very chummy,* she thought. *Extremely chummy, in fact, with her arm draped on his shoulder.* She forced herself to look away and return to the lively table conversation between the sisters.

"Well, I think I've finally extracted poor Coop from Dr. Kiki's clutches," Weezie was saying to no one in particular.

"Weezie! What did you do?" Ava frowned at her much younger

sibling, whom she had always treated more like a daughter than sister.

"Nothing, Mommy Dearest. Coop and I have been out a couple of times, that's all."

"Kiki's fine," Gail said. "Once you get to know her, she's really nice."

Weezie rolled her eyes. "You don't have to work closely with her all day long. She thinks she's entitled to look over my shoulder and evaluate everything I do *for the good of the horses*. It's bullshit, of course, but Gus, Dennis, and even Dad let her get away with it. No one respects my opinion or experience."

Gail smiled at her sister. "That's because Dad wants you to finish grad school. Not because he doesn't trust you."

"I hear great things about your pony camps. A lot of my students have younger brothers and sisters who love coming to Morgan's Fire," Greta said.

"Thank you, Greta. At least someone appreciates me!"

"Now, that's not fair," Pam said. "We all appreciate you and respect you. That includes Dad, Gus, Dennis, *and* Kiki."

"If you believe that you are the queen of Fantasyland," Weezie said, gazing up, eyes scanning the room. "Oh, my God!"

They all turned in the direction of Weezie's gaze in time to see Kiki Bloom on the arm of village blacksmith, Coop Merrick, as the couple headed into the bar.

"Well, that's it. He's history," Weezie said, spearing a piece of the thinly sliced swordfish pastrami.

Greta couldn't be certain, but she thought she spied tears rimming Weezie's chocolate-brown eyes. *I know that feeling,* she thought. *Join the club.* She had lost sight of Murph and his comanager, but she had no doubt they were somewhere wrapped around each other. Thus she was startled by his deep voice behind her. "Good evening, ladies. How's your dinner?"

"Terrific," Ava said as the sisters all chimed in.

Greta turned and gazed up at him. "Hello."

"Hi. Welcome back."

Her heart was in her throat, but Greta managed to sputter, "Thanks. I agree with the general consensus. Everything has been incredible."

"You having dessert?" he asked, gazing around the table. "We're doing ice cream on the deck tonight—cones or cups. Flavors at the bottom of the dessert menu."

"I'm in!" Weezie said. "What do you say, ladies?"

The chorus of yeses rang out as Lyddie arrived, Murph momentarily forgotten.

"Well, I'll leave you to it," he said, stepping back with one furtive look at Greta.

GRETA SAT NEXT TO PAM, LICKING A DELICIOUS PEPPERMINT STICK ICE cream cone and listening to the good-natured chatter of the sisters. The scent of honeysuckle, beach roses, and the sea wafted by on evening breezes. A perfect evening except for the weird encounter with Murph that had left her emotions churning. "Hey, you okay?" Pam asked, touching her arm.

"Yes... No. I don't know. This has been really fun being with you all, but seeing Murph has really done a number on me."

"He is acting kind of weird," Pam said. "If it makes you feel any better, Sandy says he's been off all summer, so don't take it personally."

"I've got to let go of hope there. As far as men go, I'm hopeless."

"Don't give up. Mr. Right will come along. What about my brother? You guys seemed to hit it off."

"Gorgeous doctor who lives hundreds of miles away? Out of my league and geography."

Pam laughed. "Don't look now, but Mr. O'Neill is headed this way, and he only has eyes for you."

Greta stood. "Well, I'm going to the fabulous designer ladies' room." She hurried off the deck in the opposite direction before

Murph reached the table. Pam was not surprised to see him change direction and practically run after her.

"Hey, baby," her husband said, bending to kiss her cheek. "Was that my flaky manager running off?"

She nodded. "He's trying to catch Greta."

"I hope he doesn't mow down a customer on his way. Thank God we have Rori. If he wasn't my best friend, I'd have fired his ass," he whispered, then straightened up. "Evening, ladies. How was everything?"

"Incredible."

"Fabulous."

"The best!"

Gail looked up at her brother-in-law, smiling. "The other area restaurants are going to hate you for taking their business, you know."

He shrugged. "We're small enough that I don't think we'll hurt anyone. Besides, like it or not, the area is growing. With Barnum's Ledge and the new developments going in up river, there'll be plenty of business for everyone."

"Well, no matter what, you've got a winner here," Ava said, raising her ice cream cone to him. "Our dinner really was out of this world."

"Thanks. Meryl's pretty talented," he said. "Enjoy your ice cream, all handmade here. I'd better check on things inside."

As he headed off, Ava looked at Pam. "What's the story with Greta and Murph? That was a little strange."

Pam threw up her hands. "Who knows, but I wish they'd fix it."

Greta barely made it to the ladies' room before she burst into tears. She hurried in past the sea-foam tiled wall of water and into one of the luxurious stalls, each with its own toilet, sink, and vanity area, complete with a stool and trifold mirror. She closed the door, plopped on the stool, and put her head in her hands, sobbing. A minute later, she heard a knock on the stall door.

"Hey, it's me. Can we talk?"

Lifting her head she stared at the door. "Murph?"

"Yeah, let me in, will you?"

"You're in the ladies' room!"

"Tell me about it. Now please open the door, Greta."

She grabbed a tissue and dried her eyes, then unlatched the door. Murph stepped in and closed and latched it behind him.

"Oh, geez, you've been crying. I'm so sorry."

"Don't be. It's clear you've moved on, and I need to as well."

"Moved on? What are you talking about?"

She shook her head. "Nothing...everything. It doesn't matter. We're just friends. You can be with anyone you choose."

He took hold of her arms. "I'm not with anyone Greta. I promise."

"What about your comanager? You two seem pretty cozy."

"We get along, thank God, but that's work. We work well together."

She stepped back. "Okay, this is ridiculous. We are not having this conversation in the ladies' room." She turned and grabbed her purse, trying to scoot around him.

"I've missed you," he said, arms now at her waist, drawing her closer. "Can't we at least have a friendly welcome-home hug?"

In answer, Greta circled her arms around his neck, breathing in his comforting woodsy scent. Before she knew it, they were kissing. *Definitely more than a friendly welcome-home kiss!* As the kiss deepened, he pulled her to him, his back now against the cool tiled wall. "Oh, baby," he growled, his hands reaching up to cup her breasts.

Greta felt his erection pressed against her tummy, and she sighed, beginning a rhythmic rubbing and caressing with her hips. She knew with certainty where this was leading, until a knock at the stall door interrupted them. "Hello, anyone in there?"

"Just a sec," Greta called. "Now what?" she whispered. "How embarrassing is this?"

He grinned. "I'm glad we're still friends."

"Ha-ha," she said. "Now let me pass."

"I'll call you," he said, as she opened the door to find a startled woman staring at them. "Problem with the sink," he said as they hurried out of the room.

When Greta returned to the table, the sisters were preparing to depart. The wind had picked up, and everyone was fleeing the deck. "So?" Pam asked as they walked out.

"Who knows?" Greta replied. "If anything, I'm more confused than ever, but that was one of my most memorable trips to the ladies' room ever!"

CHAPTER 34

Greta woke to the howl of wind and the phone's ringing.

It was Pam. "Hey, how are you doing up there?"

"Slept like a log, but the wind's sure picked up."

"It's bad, Greta. The forecast says the hurricane will hit us full force at high tide."

"You're kidding."

"No. Turn on the weather while you still have power. I'm calling because residents of River Road are being advised to evacuate. Sandy and I are going to the farm. There are plenty of bedrooms and lots of space in the sunroom. I think you should come be with us. You're so exposed up there."

"I'll be fine, but if things get rough, I'll call you."

"I really think you should head over here as soon as possible."

"You're probably right, but what would I do with Daisy? I can't leave her here."

"Bring her. There's plenty of room in the barn."

"Not sure your Dad would agree."

"It was him that suggested I call you."

"Well, let me get things battened down here, and I'll head down in a bit. What time is it supposed to hit us?"

"Shortly after noon."

"Plenty of time, then. I'll call when I'm on my way."

Greta hung up and took Daisy out in the backyard. The little goat was almost lifted off her feet by a strong gust of wind, and Greta had trouble staying upright. After putting out fresh food, water, and hay and encouraging Daisy to go into the shed to eat, she crossed the yard and went through the east gate that led to the water. When she reached the edge of the embankment, she grasped a tree branch to steady herself and peered over the edge. The sea was a writhing mass of white. Enormous waves crashed against the beach below. As she stood watching in horror, a huge wave rolled in, its spray drenching her. When it retreated, it looked like it took half the beach with it.

Letting go of her branch, she fought her way back to the gate and found Daisy bleating wildly, her hooves banging against the fence. "Hey, girl, it's okay. We're getting out soon."

She hurried to secure the terrace furniture and any loose equipment and tools in the backyard. She brought some of the furniture into the house; the rest she stowed in the shed or tied down. The wind continued its ceaseless howling as she hurried inside to pack an overnight bag. The work had taken longer than she expected, and when she looked at the kitchen clock, it was eleven forty-five. "Shit!" she said aloud. "I forgot your food, Daisy!"

She opened the slider, then shut it, leaving the goat inside as she fought her way across the backyard. Sea spray crested the fence, and she could see breakers at the edge of the bank. Quickly, she grabbed grain and oats and decided they'd have everything else at the farm. Chiding herself for waiting so long, she ran back to the house and locked the slider behind her. Drenched, she threw off her wet clothes by the washer and ran into the bedroom for dry jeans, sneakers, and a jersey. Everything she was taking was by the front door. *Now to get all this and Daisy to the truck!*

The little goat tried to push ahead, but Greta nudged her back, throwing the bags and baskets on the porch, then following after them and shutting the door behind her. "I'll be right back, sweetie," she called above the roar of the wind. She threw everything into the cab of the truck and went back to collect Daisy. Menacing black clouds hovered over them as she carried her pet out to the truck. As Greta set her down and turned to open the door, the leash slipped out of her hand, and that was all it took.

"Daisy!" she cried as the tiny goat took off down the driveway, instantly disappearing in sheets of rain. Only then did Greta notice their surroundings. Waves were now cresting over the cliffs, obscuring the road under their roiling, foamy assault. *We're trapped*, she thought as she ran after Daisy, knowing it was dangerous and foolish. As she fought her way through the shallow swirling water, she caught glimpses of the goat before she vanished again in the mist.

As Greta caught hold of a tree at the side of the road, she realized she would have to turn back. Tears streaming down her face, she began to fight her way toward the cottage. Several times, she lost her footing and was carried across the road, where she grabbed anything she could to prevent being taken by the receding wave. When she reached her driveway, a wave crashed over her, and Greta wrapped her arms tightly around a telephone pole, holding on for dear life. As the driveway flooded, she wondered if she could even make it back to the house. Frantically, she looked around for objects to grab hold of as she clawed her way toward the truck. The nearest object was a decorative fence that appeared to be teetering in the onslaught.

It's that or nothing, she thought, waiting to push off on the receding tide. Finally, she let go of the pole and pushed forward, step by step, in the wind. Wires danced above her, loose and menacing. *If I don't get pulled out to sea, there's always electrocution*, she thought as she reached the fence and grabbed hold.

Her assessment had been correct. The fence was loose and wouldn't hold long. As she gazed about for her next handhold she decided it would have to be the truck. Just as she prepared to launch herself, the fence broke loose from the ground, taking her with it as a wave pulled them seaward. Wild with terror, she looked around for anything that might save her, but saw nothing but roiling sea, pounding rain, and swirling mist. She clawed the ground as she neared the embankment, knowing with certainty that if she was pulled over, she would not survive in the maelstrom below. *Please,*

please, this can't be it! she thought as the last pieces of fence shattered in her hands.

Since early morning, Sandy, Murph, and the crew worked to secure the restaurant and cover the windows with plywood. It was after eleven when they completed the battening down, and the two friends walked out together, the wind whistling all around them. Field and Fire sat on a cliff far above the sea, so it would mostly be safe except for damage from wind and flying debris. All the outdoor furniture was now stored inside. They'd done as much as they could.

"Where are you headed?" Sandy asked.

"Home, I guess," Murph said.

"You're welcome to come to the farm. I'm sure Callie's made enough food for an army, and we'll all be there. Pam just called, and she's on her way. Meryl's coming too, because they evacuated River Road."

"Well, if you're sure? It would be nice not to have to ride this out alone."

"Come on, follow me."

They arrived at Morgan's Fire shortly before noon and spied a number of cars and trucks. As the friends parked and headed in, Sandy yelled above the wind, "This looks to be a campout-in-the-sunroom night." The farmhouse had a sunporch, the windows now boarded up, that ran the length of the second floor. The brainchild of Richard Morgan and modeled after the sunroom they'd had in Maine, the room was lined with comfortable couches and chairs. A perfect spot for relaxing with a good book or camping out.

"Yeah, the gang's all here!" Richard cried as the two walked into the enormous first-floor family room. Ava and Dan Fielding and their three kids were playing in one of the alcoves. Although cavernous, the room felt warm and inviting, with fires blazing in stone fireplaces at both ends. There were several seating areas with sectionals and chairs, and one corner area, where the Fieldings now played, was furnished with smaller chairs, bookshelves, and bins of toys. Gail and Pam sat with Lucy and her mother, Helen, in one of the other seating areas, along with Helen's friend Frankie Brown, a River Road evacuee. Others were seated here and there in conversation.

"Where's Tim?" Sandy asked his sister.

"Down helping at Land's End," Gail said. "He says he's coming here, but I begged him to stay put till the storm's over."

Pam looked up at her husband. "I'm worried about Greta. She should have been here by now, and she's not answering her phone."

"Geez," Sandy said. "We just saw Pete Avery, Bobby Moniz, and some of the other local cops on our way through town, and they say the Coast Road has washed out. They're not even sure Sandy's will make it."

Heart in his throat, Murph listened. "That means she's stranded up there."

"The cottage has been there a long time. If she stays put, she'll probably be okay," Sandy said, eying his friend.

"I'll be back," Murph said, turning to go.

"No way, buddy," Sandy cried, running after him all the way to his truck. "In order to get to her, you'd be going straight into it." He grabbed Murph's arm. "It's suicide, man."

"No way I'm leaving her up there alone. I know a back way."

"You mean Pettrey's Farm? That's totally overgrown and impassable."

"We'll see, won't we," Murph said, shrugging out of his friend's grasp.

"You're crazy! Good luck!" Sandy yelled as Murph slammed the door and headed off.

Dodging wires everywhere, he made it through town and onto inland back roads that ran parallel to the Coast Road. Finally, he reached the old Pettrey farmlands abandoned years earlier and left to grow wild. There were a number of trails and paths running all over the acreage, and Murph knew most from riding dirt bikes and ATVs in there as teenagers. Sheltered from the wind by huge trees, he said a silent prayer that one of the old elms, oaks, or maples wouldn't decide to topple over and kill him or block the way. When he finally emerged on the Coast Road, the road had disappeared under the waves that now crashed over it.

"Shit," he said as he headed the truck along the side of the road, keeping to high ground wherever he could, dodging trees, branches, and all manner of flying debris.

Suddenly, he stopped to watch a mound of dark black-and-white wash across the road. "Daisy!" he cried, hopping out and fighting the water to grab her up, hoping she was still alive.

As he lifted her in his arms, she turned her head and gave a weak bleat. "Come on, baby. Now where the hell is your mistress?"

Murph wrapped the goat in a blanket and drove forward, still a good half mile from the cottage. "Please be there," he said aloud, fearful that she had ventured out in search of her pet and been sucked into the maw. Finally, he dared go no further and parked on high ground, grabbing a rope from the back. After securing one end to his front bumper and the other end around his waist, he headed off into the swirling torrent, unable to see more than two feet in front of him. With every incoming wave, he was knocked to the ground, and then righted himself and pushed onward. *Please be inside, Greta. 'Cause there's no way you could survive out here.*

Arms and legs scratched raw, her jeans torn to shreds by the pavement, Greta felt herself losing the fight. She stumbled and came up with a briny mouthful of saltwater. Any minute, the surf would suck her forward and over the cliffs into the deadly roiling ocean. Suddenly through the mist, strong hands grabbed her.

"Greta, what the hell!" Murph cried as he swooped her into his arms.

He had roped himself to his truck parked down the road. He now wrapped it around Greta's waist as well. Tied together with her, he began the slow fight back to the truck, the sea spray stinging his eyes, sheets of water slapping his cheeks, cutting like knives. Each pull of the rope advanced them a few feet. Several times, waves knocked them over, but Murph held fast and righted them, spitting out mouthfuls of murky water as he pushed onward. Shivering, Greta wrapped her arms around his neck and held on tight.

He had parked on a crest and so the truck was still above water. As they reached the rise, he yanked them both to safety and held on to the truck while he untied her. Greta collapsed into his arms, sobbing. "Daisy! I lost her, Murph. She's gone, and it's all my stupid fault. I should have left hours ago and—"

He stopped her words with a quick kiss as he reached around and opened the door. There, tied to the seat, was the little goat, covered with a blanket. Greta hopped in, and he followed, slamming the door against the howling wind.

"Oh, Murph, you found her," she cried, wrapping her arms around his neck.

"More importantly, I found you, and I'm never, ever letting you go." He kissed her lightly, then settled her into the passenger seat. "We're continuing this later, but right now, we've gotta get out of here. This is far from over!"

Waves lapped at the truck's tires as Murph backed up. The Coast Road had disappeared, lost in the surging sea. Greta shivered beside him, cradling Daisy. The little goat trembled, but lay still as Greta cooed to her. Murph turned inland away from the water and the raging sea, and they were soon in the woods and fields, the way forward a thick cloud of blowing debris that pelted the truck's hood and windshield. They made slow, steady progress and were soon on the Bayport Pike only two miles north of Morgan's Fire. As he turned in the drive, he said, "We're here. You okay?"

"More than okay," she whispered, kissing the top of Daisy's head.

CHAPTER 35

The storm calmed by evening. Power was out all over the peninsula, but Richard's generator kept the farmhouse light-filled and warm. After a huge meal, houseguests retired early after the exhausting day. People fanned out to sleep all over the house. Lucy lent Greta some pajamas and clothes, and they settled Daisy in the barn with Weezie's four goats. Greta had her own room, and Murph camped out in the sunroom. Murph walked her to her room, their first moments alone since the truck. "Thank you," she said softly, her arms circling his strong shoulders.

In answer, he captured the lips he loved in a deep, lingering kiss. "My pleasure," he whispered, his voice husky as they came up for air. "I'd give anything to follow you right into your room and hold you all night, but I'll be a good boy. Night." He kissed her forehead and released her.

The following morning, Callie set out an enormous breakfast buffet, and people came and went all morning. On her second mug of excellent coffee, Greta was chatting with Lucy, Richard, Gail, Weezie, and Pam as she finished her breakfast when Murph came in, filling a plate and sitting beside her. "Morning," he said, first to her, then her companions. "Where's the boss?"

"He left an hour ago," Pam said. "Wanted to check on Maisie and then he's coming back to see how the restaurant fared. You'd never know it here with Dad's high-powered generator, but the power's out all over the village."

"Fortunately, Field and Fire also has a generator," Richard said. "'Twas a good investment."

Murph ate quickly, thanking Callie for a thermos of coffee to go. "I've gotta head out soon. Anyone need a ride?"

"I'd love a ride home, but I don't want to take you out of your way. Plus I have no idea what I'll find at the cottage."

Murph gazed down at her, his eyes soft. "I'm happy to take you."

Weezie rose, grabbing a muffin as she prepared to head out. "Why don't you leave Daisy here. I just checked on the goats, and she's fine."

"Thanks, that would be really helpful," Greta said as she prepared to go.

"Would you like coffee to go as well?" Callie asked.

"Thanks, but two cups is plenty for me," Greta said. "Thank you all for everything. Lucy, I'll wash your things and get them back to you."

"No hurry," her hostess said. "I hope you find things okay at home. Fingers crossed."

A soft wind blew as they walked to the truck holding hands. After hopping in the truck, Murph turned to her. She looked tired and drawn—not surprising—but still possessed the ethereal beauty he loved with all his heart. If he'd had any doubt, the previous day had erased it. He knew that if he had lost her, he would have gone mad. "Mind if I stop at the restaurant first?"

"Of course not," she said, giving him a wan smile.

As they drove up the long drive past the winery, tree branches were down everywhere. In several places, he had to drive off-road around large limbs. A huge oak lay in the center of the winery's circular entry drive. It had just narrowly missed the tasting barn. Field and Fire had sustained a fair amount of damage to the grounds, but the building looked fine. They walked around the building to find the deck in pieces.

"Geez, that had to be the wind or maybe a water spout?"

"You mean a little twister?"

He nodded. "They come across the water once in a while. I'm sure a hurricane churns up a bunch of them. I'll call and see how soon a crew can get over here."

They rounded the building just as Sandy drove up. "Morning! How's it look?" he called.

"Deck's trashed, but otherwise, the building seems fine. We'll see when the plywood comes off how the windows fared. I'll call Zeke and see how soon he can get a crew out. I'm guessing they'll be swamped, so it may be a while." Zeke Snyder and his Cove Construction crew had built the restaurant and three-quarters of most of the new construction in the village.

"Have you driven through town?" Greta asked.

Sandy nodded. "Just came from River Road. All the houses came through, but a couple lost their docks. Same thing at the fishery. Big tree down on Netherfield Manor. My ex-mother-in-law's in a tizzy. Apparently, it did a lot of damage to her million-dollar slate roof."

"Maisie and Lolly okay?" Murph asked.

"Yup. Jack's with 'em. What's your plan for the day?"

"I'm taking Greta home, then whatever you need. Are we opening for dinner?"

His friend shook his head. "Much as I'd like to, people need to be home cleaning up their own places. We'll try for tomorrow. If you call Zeke, that's enough for now. And listen, if you're headed up the Coast Road, be careful. Big chunks of it are gone, and it's pretty impassable. I rode out to Sandy's to check it out. They lost all the decks and two of the sheds, but miraculously, the main building survived. It took quite a beating."

They talked for a few minutes, then Murph and Greta turned to go. "I'll check back," he said.

"No hurry. I'm guessing there may be some cleanup at Greta's." Sandy waved and headed inside.

∾

Sandy hadn't exaggerated. The Coast Road was mostly gone. Chunks of pavement lay at odd angles along the cliffs and the side of the road, and trees were down everywhere. Murph drove slowly around each new obstruction. "It's like an obstacle course," he muttered, "except there's no rhyme or reason to how the obstacles are placed."

"Are you sure this is a good idea?" she asked. "We could have gone up the Bayport Pike, then back down to get to my place."

He shrugged. "I kinda wanted to see Sandy's and this area. It'll be fine. Almost there."

Finally, they rounded the corner, and the cottage came into view. It was there and appeared to be unscathed except for the fence. Her truck had been swept out of the driveway and into a neighbor's field. "Do you think it'll still run?" she asked softly.

"We'll check it out and see." Murph parked on the side of the road at the edge of the driveway, and they headed up the front walkway, now in disarray with flagstones strewn across the yard.

The interior of the house seemed fine, but a dampness hung in the air. Greta opened the cellar door and shone a flashlight into the dark. The floor was under at least four inches of water. "This is when I kick myself for not buying a generator. There's no way for me to get the sump pump going."

"I can bring one from my house. Better you have it. My house should be fine except for wind damage. Come on, let's check the yard."

A few small trees were down, and plantings had been flattened by the wind and rain as well as the saltwater spray. It did not appear that the waves had breached the yard, stopping short on the other side of the fence.

"The fence is still up, thank goodness," she said. "I can bring Daisy home."

The shed door hung at an odd angle, ripped by the wind. "Why don't I grab of few of your dad's tools and fix the shed door, then help you clean up a little before I go?"

"Only if you have time. Can we check the truck first?"

"Of course. Got the keys?"

They walked to the field, and she got in. Her first attempt to start it failed. The engine sputtered and died. "Everything's probably soaked," he said. "Pop the hood, and I'll have a look."

After a few minutes of poking around, he popped his head up. "Yup, she's soaked. Sun's out, so let's leave the hood up. After we clean up, we can try again."

Sure enough, several hours later, after repairing the shed and cleaning the debris out of the front yard and driveway, they tried again, and the Tacoma sputtered to life. Greta drove it up the drive and parked as Murph followed on foot.

"Thank you," she said walking to meet him, holding out her arms to hug him.

His strong arms held her tight for several minutes before he said, "I should really head over to Field and Fire, but why don't I check back later. Who knows when the power will be restored. If it's still out later, I'll grab my generator to power up your sump pump. I could also pick up some dinner?"

"What makes you think you can find any place open?"

"Let me worry about that. See you around six?"

"Thanks," she said wearily.

"Get some rest. I'll stop and get Daisy at the farm if you like, or would you rather she stay there till tomorrow?"

"No, I'd love it if you'd bring her home. See you later, then." She waved as he drove off, then walked back to the house and collapsed on the living room sofa. *I'm home and safe*, she thought as she drifted off to sleep.

CHAPTER 36

Murph stopped by Field and Fire on his way home and found Rori and Meryl chatting in the kitchen. "Hey, ladies, anything you need from me?"

"We're good," Rori said. "My house lost its dock, but otherwise, it's fine."

"Yeah?" he said.

"Yup, the owners think they can retrieve it down river and reattach it."

"Good luck with that."

"To answer your question," Meryl said. "Since the boss has given us the night off and the crew just finished the windows, we're all set. I'm gonna do some prep and then head home."

"Zeke's already been here?"

Rori nodded. "Briefly. He's busy running around town giving estimates to people about work, but three of his guys pulled off the plywood, stored it in the winery barn, and washed the windows. Zeke said they can get to the deck by early next week."

"Great. Meryl, I have a favor. Have you got anything prepped that you could give me for dinner for two?"

"I have some beautiful fresh salad and swordfish kabobs all ready for the grill. If you stop for some bread, you'd have your meal. There are also berry flans in the fridge."

"Perfect. Can I pick things up around five thirty?"

Meryl smiled. "They'll be in a to-go bag in the first fridge if I've gone."

"Thanks, Meryl. You're a peach!"

"Good luck, Romeo!" Rori called, winking at Meryl as Murph hurried out the back door.

His house was in great shape except for a few branches down. He did a little yard work, showered, loaded up the generator and a can of gas, and headed back out. He wanted to make a quick run home to check on his parents and pick up something his mom promised to have ready for him. Their little farm had weathered the storm just fine. His dad was out clearing the fields and checking on the livestock, but his mom greeted him with open arms. He sat chatting for a short while, then rose to go. Fiona O'Neill pressed the small velvet box into his hand. "Good luck, darlin'."

"Thanks, Mum," he said, embracing her.

HE ARRIVED JUST BEFORE SIX, THE BASKET OF MERYL'S FOOD IN ONE hand, a good bottle of wine in the other, and Daisy on a leash at his side. In jeans and a collared summer sports shirt, he looked good enough to eat, never mind the dinner, Greta thought. She had showered and changed into slacks and a light summer sweater. The color, a creamy mauve, brought out the flecks of sunlight in her violet eyes. She wore silver teardrop earrings and a matching bracelet.

"You look lovely," he said as she bent to pet the goat, fussing over her.

"Thanks for bringing her home."

"My pleasure. Now I'll put these things down, and I can install the generator."

It was a quick job because there was a generator hookup in the basement. Soon the sump pump was chugging along, and the cottage was bathed in soft light. Murph came up to wash his hands in the kitchen sink.

"Thank you," she said softly.

"My pleasure. Want me to start the grill for the kabobs?"

"It's gas, so it's very quick. Why don't we have a drink first?"

He asked for beer, and she opened the sauvignon blanc he brought and poured a glass for herself. She brought a small platter of cheese, crackers, and vegetables out to the terrace, where the table was set for two. They sat side by side on the porch glider, swinging gently as they chatted about the day, the storm damage in the village, and a variety of small talk. Their conversation felt easy, but there were sparks in the air between them.

A lull in the conversation found them gazing out at Daisy playing in the yard. Greta said, "Shall we start the grill?"

Abruptly, Murph stood and held out his hand. "Take a walk with me first."

She reached out to him, always loving the feel of his rough but gentle hands. "Okay."

CHAPTER 37

He led her around the house and out the side gate, making sure to latch Daisy inside. "We'll be right back, girl, I promise," he said, reaching down to pet the downy head.

Greta laughed. "I think she likes you better than me. Where are we off to, anyway?"

"You'll see. By the way, I meant to tell you earlier. I'll come by on my next day off and help you put up a new fence out here," he said, waving at the front yard, which was still covered with branches and debris. "That is if you want to replace it?"

"Honestly, I haven't thought that far ahead, but thanks. I'd love the help once I figure things out." She squeezed his hand as they started walking along the rutted, washed-out section of the Coast Road. It was passable, but dangerous, with deep holes, ruts, and chunks of pavement strewn everywhere.

Finally, he stopped and took her hands. "Recognize where we are?"

An involuntary shudder passed through her as she nodded. "Where you saved me from being washed out to sea."

As he shook his head, his eyes met hers. "It's where I saved myself and you saved me. I knew in that moment that I could never let you go again. I love you, Greta. I'm a screwed-up mess, but I love you more than anything in the world. I've known that since I spied you running around after that crazy goat of yours. I just couldn't admit it. Couldn't let myself feel that unconditional, can't-breathe-without-you, joined-at-the-hip, forever kind of love, even though it's always been there. I was just too scared."

Suddenly, Murph went down on one knee on the muddy, damp road, looking up, a tiny green box in one hand. "Gosh, feels great to get this out of my pocket. It's been poking me since I picked it up."

Greta gazed down, eyes wide in astonishment. "Murph, you're going to be soaked. You're kneeling in a puddle."

"Don't care. I'd kneel in quicksand to say what I have to say. Greta Jeffers, I adore you and cannot imagine another day of life without you in it. I've missed you every second since we've been apart. The last two months have been agony. What I'm trying to say is that I'm far from perfect, but I promise to spend every day trying my best to make you happy.

"I don't expect you to say yes, but I wanted to ask—will you marry me? You can think about it for days, weeks, months, years. Hell, as long as you want, and I'll keep going to therapy and working at not being so crazy and—"

"Yes," she said.

"You didn't say no? Then you'll think about it?"

"I don't have to think about it, Murphy O'Neill. I've loved you since I first met you with Sandy and Pam. Unfortunately, you were attached to someone else back then. I'm saying yes, I'll marry you! I'd love to marry you anytime, anywhere. Now stand up so I can kiss you, please."

Hopping up, Murph pulled her to him, capturing her lips in a sensual deep kiss, their tongues entwined, desperately needing each other. As Greta grew weak-kneed and feared she might fall, she pulled back and peeked up at him. "Aren't you going to show me what's in the box?"

His smile melted her heart as he opened the little green box to reveal a lovely vintage ring, the diamond accented with a fleur-de-lis pattern, pale blue sapphires on the sides. "It was my grandmother's. If it's not your style, we can get another one."

"It's perfect," she said, holding out her hand as he slipped it on her finger. "And it fits perfectly too."

He smiled. "I had Lyddie borrow one of the rings I know you wear so the jeweler could size it."

"So this wasn't a snap decision? You've been planning this, huh?"

"Planning, yes, executing it, not so sure when, until I saw you about to get swept away from me. I knew I couldn't wait another day. My mother picked it up last week and was keeping it safe until today. Now I intend to keep you safe forever."

"I'm glad," she said, hugging him. "Are you hungry?"

"Hungry for you."

Greta laughed. "First things first."

"That's exactly right! First things first," he said, sweeping her up in his arms and carrying her into the house.

Once inside, he set her down, their hands everywhere, clothes flying as they slowly made their way toward the bedroom. Both were naked when they reached the bed and lay down, wrapped around each other. Murph had protection at hand as he caressed her with his hands, then lips and tongue, moving down to part her smooth, silky legs, finding her wet and so ready for him. "What do you want, babe?"

"You, inside me, now."

"Your wish is my command." He sheathed himself and moved over her, finding her soft warm center. He moved gently at first, then with hungry urgency as she matched his every thrust. Commencing a dance they already knew well, they waltzed together as one to a crashing, explosive climax.

Breathless and sated, Greta kissed him lightly. "Oh, I've missed that," she sighed.

"Me too. You have no idea. I love you so much, babe."

"Me too," Greta whispered, nibbling his shoulder in a playful kiss. "And to think we can do this all the time now, anytime, anywhere."

He rolled them to lie side by side, kissing her playfully. "You got that right, fiancée. Is it time to tell Daisy the good news?"

Read on for sample chapters of *A Horseshoe Crab Cove Christmas*, book seven of the Morgan's Fire series.

A HORSESHOE CRAB COVE CHRISTMAS

Chapter 1

Main Street looked magical with its twinkling Christmas lights and wreath-bedecked street lamps laced with snow. Soft puffy flakes covered Joe's hat and jacket, some settling on his eyelashes, blurring his vision. He blinked them away, wondering if he would ever see clearly again.

Two weeks earlier, Joseph O'Leary, priest at St. Mary's by the Sea, had walked away from his life's work. He had loved being a priest. Saying goodbye had been excruciating, but he knew he wanted a different life, a spiritual life, but one that held the possibility of a wife and family. The dream was there, and after two years of struggle, he knew he could not let it go. Tonight, geography was on his mind. He must move out of the parsonage to make way for Father Flynn. He didn't know where life would eventually take him, but Bayport, home to St. Mary's, might be too close right now. Hence his solo walk down the snowy street in Horseshoe Crab Cove. After grabbing a coffee at the Crab Café, he headed to the village's community garden at the far end of Main Street. As he strolled, the soft light from the shops and their festive window displays warmed his heart. *Such a beautiful season*, he thought. *So full of hope and joy.*

He sighed as he passed through the gate into Laura's Community Garden. The raised beds were now covered with straw, ornamental cabbage and hardy spinach poking through their winter blankets. He'd visited the garden before and always found it to be a deeply spiritual place. Walking to the far end, he brushed snow from a teak bench and sat, the quiet surrounding him.

He sipped his coffee in the growing twilight. Gradually, the snow let up and the lights draping garden fences and trees came on. *Maybe I can make a home here*, he mused, *until I decide upon next steps.*

An elderly couple strolled through the front gate and headed for a plot at the garden's south end. They held tight to each other as they shuffled along, finally pausing at a bed that appeared completely bare until the woman reached down, then straightened up with a handful of crimson blooms. She smiled, offering them to her companion, his expression beatific as he stared at the flowers, then bent to kiss her cheek. As Joe watched, he realized that tears clouded his vision and streamed down his cheeks. Brushing them aside, he was surprised to see the couple approaching.

"Good evening," she said. "Lovely night, isn't it? Nathanial, I believe we've found a kindred spirit who loves the winter garden as much we do."

Joe stood, nodding to them. "It is, indeed, a beautiful spot. May I ask what those flowers are that bloom in the snow?"

"Our winter camellias," she said. "My Nathanial's favorite."

Her companion remained silent, a slight smile on his face as his eyes darted about. Joe recognized the misty confusion of dementia and thought how lucky the man was to have such a loving companion. "They're lovely," Joe said.

She adjusted Nathanial's brightly colored scarf and purple wool beret against the cold, then smiled up at Joe. "Do you live in the village?"

"Not yet. I live in Bayport, but I'm considering a move."

"You won't be sorry."

"I expect that's true," Joe said, walking alongside them to the front gate.

"I'm Elizabeth, and this is my husband, Nathanial."

"Joe."

"Well, here we are," she said, indicating a small sedan in the hardware store lot. "Can we offer you a lift?"

"Thanks, but my car's just up the street."

"Well then, good night, Father Joe. I do hope you settle in our tiny piece of heaven. We'll enjoy seeing you around town. Take care."

With those surprising words, she turned and led her husband off, leaving Joe to stare after them. *Small towns.* Of course they'd have attended services at St. Mary's over the years—weddings, funerals, and others. He felt a twinge of guilt for not recognizing them. *Perhaps without their winter clothes, I'd have known them?*

He made his way to the truck, tossing his empty cup into a sidewalk trash bin. *Is that what I want?* he mused, brushing snow from his front windshield. *Loving companionship in my old age? Am I being selfish, abandoning my Lord and my congregation to serve my own needs?*

Chapter 2

Stunned, the O'Neills stared at their parish priest of many years. A visiting priest had given the mass that morning because Father Joseph was supposedly on vacation, but when Joe had called and asked if he might stop by, they invited him to dinner.

"Yes, I walked away," Joe said. "I wanted to tell you all first because I consider you to be family. I hope that doesn't sound presumptuous."

"Of course it doesn't, but when?" Fiona MacGregor O'Neill, the family matriarch, stared from the priest to her husband and son, Murph Junior. The latter had brought his fiancée, Greta Jeffers, to dinner.

"I wrote for dispensation six months ago. I wanted to follow process, but they said dispensation could take years, and I didn't want to wait. I'm at peace with my decision."

"Have you preached your last mass, then?"

"I'm afraid so. I wanted to tell the congregation two weeks ago, to say goodbye properly, but I was asked not to do so."

"But why?" Fiona asked, pushing aside her bowl of lamb stew.

His eyes reflected warmth and sadness as he gazed at his old friend. "It's been on my mind for several years. You may remember that I completed a degree in social work a number of years ago? To assist me in my pastoral duties. That work is calling to me. I turned fifty last winter and thought it might be time."

"This is going to sound like pure selfishness," Murph said, "but are you still able to marry us?"

Joe smiled at the young man he'd known for his entire career as a priest. The summer Murph's twin sister, Aislan, died in a tragic drowning accident had tested the priest's faith in its infancy. "I would be honored to marry you, but not in the Catholic church. At least not at St. Mary's," he added, referring to their parish church where he had presided for twenty-four years. "I'm actually standing with Anna Goodspeed, your village pastor, for the Rogers-Faulkner wedding."

Murph nodded. "I heard about that. Their reception is at Field and Fire. Our first wedding."

"So she's not having it at her mother's fancy wedding venue?" Fiona asked, referring to Cove Inn and Spa, the home of Mavis LaSalle, Lolly Rogers's mother, and one of the most sought-after event locations in New England.

Murph shrugged. "I guess they wanted Mavis to enjoy the day and not be stressed running the thing."

Turning back to their guest, Fiona frowned. "Oh, Joseph, what will we do without you?"

"The same thing you've always done. Worship as the good Catholics you are. Father Flynn will be taking my place. I've met him many times. You'll like him."

"Have you plans for the holidays?" Fiona said.

"Not yet, or should I say, they're still formulating."

"Well, you know you're always welcome here. Seamus and Darby both say they'll be home for Christmas. I'll believe that when I see it, but I know they'd love to see you."

The conversation continued over dessert, Fiona's Irish cream cheesecake, after which Joe prepared to depart. "I move out of the parsonage next weekend. Don't suppose you know of any rental properties? I'll store my things temporarily if I can't find something."

Fiona and her husband immediately offered Joe a bedroom, but before he could reply, Murph Junior interrupted. "This is your lucky day. I've moved in with Greta, so my place is free. It's been crazy busy at the restaurant with the holidays approaching, but I was going to start looking for renters after the new year. You're welcome to it for short- or long-term."

Joe looked at Murph and his beautiful fiancée. She nodded, smiling.

"Are you serious?"

"Absolutely! It's yours if you want it."

"I'll take it."

After saying goodbye to his hosts, Joe walked out with Murph and Greta, and the men arranged to meet the next morning at Field and Fire, the restaurant where Murph served as comanager. "We can drive down and look at my place then," the redhead with warm caramel eyes said as he opened his truck door for Greta. Murph owned a duplex at the south end of Horseshoe Crab Cove on the border of the neighboring town of Southport. He lived on one side and rented the other.

As he waved goodbye to the couple, Joe thought about how fortunate he was to have landed in this close knit community where help and support were never far away.

On a cool December morning at Field and Fire, the wind blew off the river. In blue jeans and green Field and Fire T-shirts, chef Meryl Stockdale and comanager Rori Lake were in the main dining room unpacking boxes of new Christmas decorations. "Thanks for the help," thirty-six-year-old Rori said, her auburn hair tied back. "But don't you have stuff to do to prep for tonight?"

Blue eyes sparkling, her sandy-blonde hair held back with a bandana, the forty-two-year-old chef gave her a look. "No worries. I've got my worker bees chopping and prepping. *This* is important. I *love* Christmas and am so excited to see the transformation of these spaces into a winter wonderland. Such cool decorations."

"Pam's department, not mine. She ordered all this. I hope she won't mind if we get started." Rori referred to the wife of owner Sandy Rodriguez, who was in charge of flowers and table arrangements.

"Well, at least we can unpack them. Oh, look at these beautiful garlands!"

As the women continued to explore the boxes, the door opened, and a tall man stepped inside, his dark brown eyes scanning the room. Meryl spied him first and smiled. Handsome, with a lean, athletic build, she guessed him to be slightly older than she, maybe late forties? "Can we help you?"

When he smiled, his craggy features aligned. *Downright gorgeous!* she mused.

"I'm meeting Murph O'Neill here. Is he in?"

Rori wrapped a long garland around her neck like a boa. "Not yet. You're Father O'Leary, aren't you? I remember you from the restaurant opening."

"Good memory," he said, "but it's just Joe. I've had a recent change in vocation."

"You've left the priesthood?" Rori asked, staring at him.

Joe nodded. "Not what I expected to discuss on this fine winter morning, but yes."

"Sorry," Rori said. "I'm kind of a lapsed Catholic, and I've been meaning to get to St. Mary's. That's where you are, or were, right?"

"That's right. Father Flynn will be taking over. He's terrific, and it's a very warm spiritual community."

Joe was aware of the other woman's gaze, her lovely blue eyes considering him with curiosity and perhaps something more? While he'd had close relationships with women parishioners over the years, Joe had always maintained professional distance. Startled, he realized that his vows of celibacy were in his past, but perhaps not in his future. *What is it about this woman?* Finally, he stepped forward, extending his hand. "Joe O'Leary."

"Oh, my bad," Rori said. "I assumed you two had met. This is our extraordinary chef, Meryl Stockdale."

Meryl took his hand, her eyes meeting his. "Pleased to meet you."

He felt heat course through him at her touch.

The front door opened, and Murph stepped in. "Hey, Joe, sorry I'm late!"

Reluctantly, he released her hand. "The pleasure's mine," he said, and turned to his young friend. "Morning. No problem, I've been chatting with your colleagues.

Get *A Horseshoe Crab Cove Christmas!*

ALSO BY M. LEE PRESCOTT

Contemporary Romance

Mystery

The Ricky Steele Mysteries

Prepped to Kill

Gadfly

Lost in Spindle City

Poof!

Lady Love: A Cautionary Tale

Also, featuring Ricky Steele:

Jigsaw

Roger and Bess Mysteries

A Friend of Silence

In the Name of Silence

The Silence of Memory

Silencing the Pen

Well-Loved Romances

Widow's Island

Hestor's Way

Morgan's Run Romances

Emma's Dream

Lang's Return

Jeb's Promise

Rose's Choice

Hope's Wonder

Ruthie's Love

Polly's Heart

Kyle's Journey

Gus' Home

A Valley Christmas

Aria's Song

Tom's Ride

Bella's Touch

Morgan's Fire Romances

Lucy's Hearth

Tim's Hands

Pam's Garden

Rich's Dilemma

Lolly's Wish

Greta's Goat

A Horseshoe Crab Cove Christmas

Joe's Calling

Young Adult Historical Romance

Song of the Spirit

A NOTE FROM THE AUTHOR

I am so happy to bring you Greta and Murph's love story! This marks the sixth of the *Morgan's Fire* books and also previews book seven, *A Horseshoe Crab Cove Christmas*. A contemporary romance series, *Morgan's Fire*, a spin-off of **Morgan's Run**, follows Helen, Harriet, Lucy, Gail, Pam, Karen, Lolly, and a host of strong, resilient women—and men—across the country to the New England coastal town of Horseshoe Crab Cove.

Thank you so much for reading *Greta's Goat (with its funny title!)* and returning to Horseshoe Crab Cove with me. I love this beautiful *fictional* village and the colorful, vibrant characters who inhabit it. If you like *Greta's Goat* and are willing to write an Amazon review, I would be very grateful. If you would like to sign up for future book releases, giveaways, and occasional notices about my books, please visit my Author Website *http://www.mleeprescott.com/* and sign up for my newsletter, then follow me on BookBub *https://www.bookbub.com/search/authors?search=M.+Lee+Prescott*. I promise I will not share your address, nor will I flood you with emails. Do visit my site to read more about my books and hear what's next.

Finally, this book has been revised, proofed, and edited many, many times, but my intrepid assistants and I are human,, so if you spot a typo, please email me at *mleeprescott@gmail.com,* and I will fix it. If you'd like to know more about my other books, please scroll ahead to the next section.

Warm wishes,

M. Lee

ABOUT THE AUTHOR

M. Lee Prescott is the author of
dozens of works of fiction for adults,
young adults, and children, among
them *Prepped to Kill*, *Gadfly*, *Lost in
Spindle City*, and *Poof!* (Ricky Steele
Mysteries), *A Friend of Silence*, *In the
Name of Silence*, and *The Silence of
Memory* (Roger and Bess Mysteries),
Jigsaw, and *Song of the Spirit*, and her
contemporary romance series,
Morgan's Run. And now book six of
Morgan's Fire, *Greta's Goat*. In

addition to her fiction, her nonfiction books are published by
Heinemann, and she has written numerous articles in the field of
literacy education. Lee is a professor emeritus at a small New
England liberal arts college, where she taught reading and writing
pedagogy. Her current research focuses on mindfulness and
connections to literacy. She regularly teaches abroad, most recently
in Singapore.

Lee has lived in southern California (love those Laguna nights!),
Chapel Hill, North Carolina, and various spots in Massachusetts and
Rhode Island. Currently, she resides in Massachusetts on a beautiful
river, where she canoes, swims, and watches an incredible variety of
wildlife pass by. She is the mother of two grown sons and spends lots
of time with them, their beautiful wives, and her beloved
grandchildren. When not teaching or writing, Lee's passions revolve

around family, yoga (Kripalu is a second home), swimming, sharing mindfulness with children and adults, and walking.

Lee loves to hear from readers. Email her at *mleeprescott@gmail.com*, and visit her website to hear the latest and sign up for her newsletters!

AUTHOR WEBPAGE AND NEWSLETTER SIGN UP
http://www.mleeprescott.com

FOLLOW ME ON BOOKBUB *https://www.bookbub.-com/search/authors?search=M.+Lee+Prescott*

Leave a review for this book.